Valentine heard the news with trepidation. Diccon Leyburn had arrived in London from the north of England and meant to take her back home with him **as** his wife, whether or not he wanted her as a woman.

Valentine told herself it was foolish to fear that Diccon could have his way. There were far too many gentlemen in town who would do anything to stop Diccon from carrying her off.

There was Martin Wakefield, for one, her handsome, radically-minded cousin. And Lord Stowe, with his fabulous fortune and golden charm. And Lord Henry Sandcroft, a gallant, fearless soldier.

Surely any one of them was a match for Leyburn—and together they would be overwhelming, Valentine assured herself.

But Valentine had much to learn about the lord who would not take no for an answer . . . and still more to learn about herself. . . .

FOOL'S MASQUERADE

SIGNET Regency Romances You'll Enjoy

FOOL'S MASQUERADE

JOAN WOLF

A SIGNET BOOK

NEW AMERICAN LIBRARY

SIGNET VISTA TRADEMARK REG.U.S. PAT. OFF. AND FOREIGN COUNTRIES
REGISTERED TRADEMARK—MARCA REGISTRADA
HECHO EN CHICAGO, U.S.A.

SIGNET, SIGNET CLASSIC, MENTOR, PLUME, MERIDIAN and NAL BOOKS
are published by
New American Library,
1633 Broadway,
New York, New York 10019

First Printing, August, 1984

1 2 3 4 5 6 7 8 9

PRINTED IN THE UNITED STATES OF AMERICA

PART I

Spring, 1809

My father had a daughter loved a man
As it might be perhaps, were I a woman,
I should your lordship.

Twelfth Night
I, iv, 121–123

1

The gray stallion snorted vigorously and I patted his powerful, arched neck. "I perfectly agree, Saladin," I said, looking around me. "This does not look like a main coaching road."

It was, in fact, the main coaching road from London to Richmond and it was quite clear to me why Mr. Speight, whose book of maps I carried, had described it as a "bonecruncher." All around there stretched grass-covered hills and wild open moors. Before me was a narrow, steep, precipitous track that led down into the pass of Coverdale. Offering up a silent prayer of gratitude that I was on the back of a horse and not riding in a coach behind one, I touched my heels to Saladin's sides and we started forward again.

In spite of the empty bleakness of the landscape I was actually quite close to my destination. "Carlton Castle," I said out loud, and Saladin's ears pricked forward at the sound of my voice. I felt a little shiver run down my backbone and grinned at my own susceptibility. Still, there isn't a schoolchild in England who wouldn't have had the same reaction. Carlton Castle was a legend, the seat of the Fitzallans, the lords of Yorkshire and for seven hundred years the greatest uncrowned family in England. Fitzallan exploits filled the history books and ran throughout chronicle, story, and ballad. The present lord was Richard Fitzallan, Earl of Leyburn, and it was toward his home of Carlton that I was journeying.

I was not, unfortunately, going in the capacity of a guest. I was, in fact, delivering a horse. Saladin, to be precise.

Saladin had come into my life at a very convenient moment. You might say he fitted my needs as neatly as I fitted his.

He was a splendid horse, strong and powerful and fast. He belonged to the Marquis of Rayleigh, owner of a famous racing stable at Newmarket, and he had the potential for greatness. Saladin had only one flaw: he would not let anyone ride him.

This presented a distinct problem for the Marquis, who had not bred the horse himself but had bought him as a three-year-old. He had paid quite a pretty penny for him, but Saladin, as he was at present, was useless. The marquis couldn't even sell him—the story of the horse's vicious temper was too well known in racing circles.

Not to put too fine a point on it, the marquis was stuck with the goods. And then one day the Earl of Leyburn had come to Newmarket for the race meeting and seen Saladin. The earl offered to buy him for a handsome price—*if* the marquis could deliver him to Carlton Castle. It is a long way from Newmarket to the moors of northwestern Yorkshire and this is where I entered the picture.

My father had been killed in Sir John Moore's retreat to Corunna a few months previously, and after three years in Portugal, I was home in England. Amid the confusion of the evacuated army, I had managed to escape the friends of my father whom I knew were filled with unwelcome plans for my future, and I headed, like a magnet to metal, to Newmarket.

If there was one thing I knew in this world it was horses. My father had been in the cavalry and I had passed the greater part of my childhood in Ireland. Papa was stationed in Kildare and I had years and years of experience galloping horses over the Curragh, that great open grassy plain that all good horses go to when they die.

I needed a job and I thought I might find one in Newmarket. I have few ordinary talents, but I can do just about anything with a horse.

I rode Saladin. He had clearly been abused as a youngster, and he was terrified of people, but we understood each other. And the marquis offered me fifty guineas to deliver him safely to Carlton.

The money was certainly attractive, especially since I had only twenty pounds between myself and starvation. And, for reasons of my own, I thought it might be a good idea to bury myself in the country for a while. I accepted the job.

The ride north had been extremely pleasant. The marquis was generous with traveling money, and Saladin and I stayed only at the best inns. I ate hearty, well-cooked meals, slept in soft comfortable beds, and best of all, had a hot bath every night. I was almost sorry to see the end of my journey in sight. I was quite certain my accommodations at Carlton Castle wouldn't be nearly as luxurious as the inns I had lately been frequenting.

I was hoping very much that I would get a position at Carlton Castle. If they hoped to do anything at all with Saladin, I thought, they would have to hire me. He would scarcely let anyone else near him.

We were deep into the pass of Coverdale by now and I looked around me with something approaching awe. On one side of me towered the enormous grassy bulk of a hillside and from all sides of me wafted the sweet smell of moorland grass and damp earth. Far in the distance I could hear the bleating of a sheep—the only sound in all that vast emptiness. I had enjoyed Portugal, its warmth, its sea; but it hadn't smelled. Too arid, I suppose. But here . . . I inhaled deeply. It was marvelous. It brought back something of my childhood in Ireland—the smell of damp, of earth and grass and bog. I hadn't realized how much I had missed it.

I followed the road toward the dale foot, through Wooddale, Bradley, and Horsehouse, where the coach horses were fed and rested. I didn't stop, however, but pushed on through the barren ramparts of grass and rock toward Carlton.

The castle was visible from quite a distance, a huge, imposing, distinctly Norman-looking bulk built to command an excellent view of the dale from all sides. I felt once again that shiver down my back. It was exactly as it should be: enormous, forbidding, feudal. Isolated. I looked around me once again. It didn't seem possible, I thought, that this quiet corner of distant Yorkshire had once been the scene of princely magnificence, of great occasions of state. Kings had visited Carlton, I knew, and most of the great names of medieval England had come and gone with steady regularity.

The Fitzallans had long since ceased to play an active role in the government of Great Britain, but the Earl of Leyburn had remained over the centuries an undisputed power in the north. The earl might make only a rare appearance in London, but no one had any doubt as to who controlled Yorkshire's vote in the Commons.

I had learned quite a bit about the Fitzallans from a young lieutenant in my father's regiment who had been stationed with us in Ireland. He was himself from Richmond and he had often joined me for a long gallop over the Curragh. It was his first posting. He was homesick and I was a good listener. And now here I was, at the very scene of Miles' many stories.

I went, not to the castle itself, but to the stables. It was late afternoon and the grooms were busy feeding. I explained who I was and who Saladin was, and the head groom told me that Lord Leyburn wasn't at home but that I had better see Mr. Fitzallan, who was his lordship's steward. I walked Saladin over to a trim grassy border and let him graze while I leaned against a neat white-railed fence and looked about me with satisfaction. The stable yard was immaculate. The stable itself was composed of two large blocks of stalls. Clearly Lord Leyburn kept quite a number of horses, which was good news for me.

"I understand you've brought Rayleigh's stallion," a calm voice said, and I pulled away from the fence and stood up straight.

"Yes, sir. This is Saladin." The stallion had stopped grazing at the man's approach, and was standing next to me. I put my hand on his shoulder and could feel how the great muscles had tensed.

"He's a beautiful animal," the man said, and looked at Saladin admiringly. I took the opportunity to study Mr. Fitzallan.

He was about thirty years of age, an enormous man at least six feet, four inches, with the widest shoulders I had ever seen. His hair was dark brown, and his eyes, when they turned to me, were very clear and blue. They were the sort of eyes you could see right into, direct, honest, and kind.

"I am Lord Leyburn's cousin and his steward," the man told me pleasantly. "His lordship wrote to me about the arrangement he made with Lord Rayleigh. I rather gathered he didn't expect Saladin to be delivered."

"I am the only one who has been able to ride him," I said earnestly. I wanted very much to impress that fact upon him. I took a deep breath. "I was hoping you would let me stay and look after him," I went on before I lost my nerve. "I'm sure I can gentle him for you. It will just take a little time."

"I see."

He looked at me speculatively and I looked bravely back, hoping he would see exactly what I wanted him to. My clothes were well worn, the breeches and jacket a little big, but otherwise they were unexceptional. They fitted my part. My hair, which is very thick and straight, I had cut in a circular fashion around my head. It was clean and shining, for I had washed it only last night. My father used to say that nature hadn't been able to make up her mind about my hair—it wasn't brown, it wasn't blond, it wasn't red, but a strange mixture of all three.

"You're rather small to be riding such a big horse," the man said.

I was five feet, five inches, and had always thought myself a rather decent height. Next to this man I felt like a midget.

"What is your age?" he went remorselessly on.

I knew I did not look like an eighteen-year-old boy. "Fifteen," I said.

"And your name?"

"Valentine Brown," I answered. The first name at least was my own.

He nodded. "Well, Valentine, I thought you were employed by the Marquis of Rayleigh."

"Oh, no, sir. That is, I never worked in his stable. He employed me only to bring Saladin north, you see."

"And now you have done that, you are out of a job."

"Yes, sir."

He nodded. "All right, I expect we can take you on. I'll speak to Hutchins."

"Ah, there is one more thing, sir," I said rather breathlessly.

He raised an eyebrow. He was a very good-looking man. "Yes?" he said. He was also a very patient man.

"I require my own room to sleep in. You see, I'm a dreadfully light sleeper and it is impossible for me to share with anyone. I'm awake the whole time."

The blue eyes narrowed and regarded me with distinctly uncomfortable shrewdness. I kept my face still, my eyes expressionless. He took a step closer to me and Saladin threw back his head and backed away. He tried to rear, but I had him firmly by the reins and began to talk to him soothingly.

"Move back," I said over my shoulder to the man, and continued to talk to the horse. After a few minutes he rubbed his face against my chest and I scratched his ears. Then I turned to look at Mr. Fitzallan.

He was standing a good ten feet away from us, and when I met his eyes, he smiled.

"I see," was all he said.

"Do I have a job?"

"You have a job. Bring the brute along to the stable and I'll give instructions to Hutchins and to Mrs. Emerson, the housekeeper up at the castle. You will have to sleep there. There are no single rooms available in the stable quarters."

I grinned in delight. I had done it! "Yes, sir. Thank you, sir." And I took Saladin off to the stable.

2

I trod warily my first week at Carlton Castle, trying to blend in with the general crowd of servants, trying not to distinguish myself in any way. I had been given a small room in the attic that contained a wardrobe, a chair, and a bed. The bed had a distinct sag in the middle, but the sheets were clean and the blankets warm. The food in the servants' hall was good and plentiful. The horses in the earl's stable were splendid. Things could have been a great deal worse.

The biggest problem I had to face that first week was fatigue. Hutchins, the head groom, had been understandably skeptical about me and the first day had ordered one of his own lads to ride Saladin. It hadn't taken the stallion a minute

17

to dump him. The lad had tried again, with the same result. Then I had gotten on. Saladin, bless him, went like a dream. My reputation was established.

I had Saladin to take care of as well as two of his lordship's hunters to groom and exercise. We were up and out on the moors at dawn for exercise gallops, then back at the stable to groom and feed and clean out stalls. In the afternoon I worked with Saladin, under the hawklike eye of Hutchins. Then there was tack to clean, horses to get in from the paddocks, horses to groom again and feed again, and finally it was time for our own dinner. I fell into bed at eight o'clock, exhausted.

I would get used to it, I told myself. According to the other lads, Lord Leyburn's was the best stable to work for in all of Yorkshire.

After I had been at Carlton a week, I had an afternoon off. I went for a walk on the moors, following a small stream that flowed behind the stable yard. It was one of those April days that promises spring, and after half an hour I picked a nice grassy spot, lay down, and went to sleep in the sun.

"If you don't get home soon, you'll miss your dinner," an amused voice said from what seemed a great distance, and I opened my eyes. An enormous shadow towered over me and I blinked in alarm and sat up.

"I'm not going to eat you, lad," the voice said mildly, and my vision cleared and I recognized Mr. Fitzallan.

"You—you startled me," I said defensively. Then, rather belatedly, "Sir."

"I'm sorry." He sat down next to me, and for the first time I noticed that he carried a gun and a game bag.

"How are you getting on, Valentine?" he asked. He put his gun down next to him and turned clear, sky-blue eyes on my face.

"Very well, thank you, sir," I replied politely. He raised an eyebrow and I felt a stab of worry. "Have—have there been any complaints?"

"No. No complaints." His blue eyes were steady on my face.

"That's good. I've been trying very hard to please."

"Too hard, perhaps."

"Sir?"

"You're not accustomed to this sort of life, are you?"

"What do you mean?" I spoke cautiously.

"Your speech," he said simply. "You speak like a gentleman."

It was so obvious and I had not thought of it. Stupid. I hoped my dismay did not show on my face. I was thinking furiously.

"My father was a gentleman," I finally said. "But he died a few months ago. There was no money and I had to earn my living. The only thing I know how to do is work with horses." All of this information was perfectly accurate, as far as it went.

"Your mother?"

"She died nine years ago."

"And you have no other family? No uncles or cousins to assist you?"

"No."

"And do you plan to remain the remainder of your life a groom?"

I shrugged. "I haven't gotten around to thinking about the rest of my life."

"I see." Then he leaned over and took my left wrist in his hand and held my hand out, palm upward. It was depressingly blistered. I bit my lip.

"I haven't complained," I said. "I do my work."

The big fingers on my wrist were strong but surprisingly gentle. Next to his hand mine looked absurdly small. He let my wrist go and I immediately clasped both my hands around my knees, effectively hiding the blisters.

"I know you do your work," he said quietly. "Hutchins tells me you are thorough and conscientious. He also says you ride like an angel."

I flushed with surprise. The only time Hutchins ever spoke to me was to issue orders. Mr. Fitzallan's words filled me with warm pleasure. I was doing a good job. I was succeeding.

I looked up at him. "There," I said. "You see?"

His eyelids flickered a little. "No, I don't see. I don't see how such an obviously gently bred boy could find himself in such an unprotected position. Didn't your father leave a will? Surely you have a guardian."

"I don't."

"Then you must be running away."

I stared straight ahead of me. "If I am not giving satisfaction, sir," I said tonelessly, "I will be on my way."

There was a long silence during which I did not look at him.

"All right," he said at last. "Have it your way. I can't in all conscience turn such an innocent out to walk the world."

I felt a little insulted to be called an innocent, but gratitude was my primary emotion. "I assure you, sir," I said earnestly, "I have told you the truth. My father is dead and there is no one alive who wants me."

He gave me a shrewd look. "Ah, but that is not what I asked you," he said. When I didn't answer, he rose to his feet. "Come. I'll walk back to the castle with you. We'll make it just in time for your dinner."

* * *

The following day Hutchins told me that the two hunters were to be given to another lad; I was to work only with Saladin. "Mr. Fitzallan wants him fit for his lordship to ride," Hutchins told me. His expressionless face gave me no clue as to his feelings.

"Yes, sir." There is no denying that I felt a sense of relief at the thought of being out from under all that hard physical labor. I just hoped my easy lot wouldn't make me universally hated in the servants' hall.

It didn't. At first I found it strange that no one seemed to resent my light schedule, but it soon became clear that the servants had divined the same thing as Mr. Fitzallan. They knew I wasn't one of them. I was Quality, and therefore it was perfectly all right for me to draw the same wage as they and yet do one quarter of the work. I rather thought their attitude was a sad comment on the English class system, but I forbore to point this out in the kitchen.

Life settled down into quite a pleasant routine. Lord Leyburn wasn't expected home for over a month and so I had a good deal of time to become comfortably ensconced in his home. The cook, Mrs. Scone, was a motherly soul who decided it was her duty in life to fatten me up. The stable lads taught me how to throw dice and I soon became very good at it. And one or two mornings a week Mr. Fitzallan requested me to accompany him on his morning ride.

On these occasions I rode one of Lord Leyburn's hunters, and at first I was wary with Mr. Fitzallan, afraid he would try to probe into what I did not want him to know. But he was easygoing and pleasant and seemed disposed to talk about any subject I introduced. I soon found myself relaxing in his company.

I liked him very much. There was a kindness in his eyes and a humorous look to his mouth that was very attractive.

"Are you Lord Leyburn's first cousin?" I asked curiously one day as we rode over the empty moor with the curlews crying overhead.

"No. My father and his father were first cousins. But both Diccon and I were only children and we grew up like brothers. I've lived here at Carlton since I left school."

"It must be exciting to belong to a family so famous in history." The wind blew my hair back from my forehead and I looked around me with satisfaction.

"I suppose. Sometimes it can be rather stifling, though."

I looked at him curiously. "How do you mean?" Gradually I had been dropping the "sir" that had originally punctuated all my comments to him.

"The Fitzallans live too much in the past," he said frankly. "They haven't approved of a monarch since King Richard was killed at Bosworth Field, and ever since then they have sulked here in the north, minding their own affairs and ignoring London."

"King Richard?" I said incredulously. "Do you mean Richard the Third? The hunchback?"

His handsome face looked suddenly stern. "Don't ever say that here in the north. Here he is 'good King Richard' and still beloved in memory. The eldest son of the Earl of Leyburn is always christened Richard in his memory."

This was astonishing news. "But Shakespeare . . ." I began.

"Shakespeare lived under a Tudor sovereign," he said. "It was in his interest to vilify Richard." I still felt unconvinced and he laughed. "I shouldn't advise you to look like that around Lord Leyburn. He can get quite violent on the subject of King Richard."

"But Bosworth Field happened in the fifteenth century," I protested.

"I know." He sighed. "That is precisely what I mean about living in the past. The world around us is changing dramatically, and we should be more aware of where we are going than where we've been."

"Yes," I said. "Why, in my own short lifetime I've seen two revolutions."

"And what were they, Valentine?" he asked gently. I looked at him and there was a long pause. "I'm not trying to catch you out," he said even more gently than before.

"No one is looking for me," I said tensely. "I swear it."

"I believe you."

I took a deep breath. "My father was in the army," I said. "We were in Ireland in '98. And in the Peninsula just recently. Papa was killed in Sir John Moore's retreat."

"I'm very sorry."

I felt an uncomfortable hard knot in my chest. "Thank you," I mumbled.

After a minute he changed the subject and gratefully I followed his lead. I didn't know what had led me to admit so much to him, but I wasn't sorry I had. He was a man to trust. I was very fortunate to have come under his charge.

3

The night after my conversation with Mr. Fitzallan I retired to my room early. I needed to do some thinking.

I pulled my boots off, cleaned them with an old cloth, and put them on the floor next to the wardrobe. Next I took off my shirt and examined it in the light of the candle. It would have to be washed. Then I untied the wide muslin sash that I had been using to bind my breasts. They were looking fuller than they had been; it seemed all of Mrs. Scone's good food had been going on in one place. I took off my breeches, hung them in the wardrobe, and pulled a nightshirt over my head. Then I got into bed under the covers. The April night was chilly.

I put my hands behind my head and stared at the ceiling. I was at a crossroad, I thought. If I stayed here at Carlton Castle, I was quite likely to be found out. Whereas if I left . . . I was quite likely to be found out that way too, I thought dismally. What had seemed a brilliant idea at the time, disguising myself as a boy and getting a job in a stable, had proved to have distinct flaws.

In point of fact, it had been an idiotic idea. The only reason I had been successful was because Mr. Fitzallan had immediately spotted me as a fraud and had taken pity on me. Oh, I didn't think he had tumbled to the fact that I was a girl, but he knew just about everything else.

I was not, strictly speaking, running away. My grandparents had never expressed the slightest interest in my welfare and, as far as I knew, would welcome me about as warmly as they would welcome the bubonic plague. They would, however, provide for me. Papa had been quite firm on that point. If anything happened to him, I was to go to Mama's parents.

My mother's parents were the Earl and Countess of Ardsley. Mother was their only child, and when she had run away with Papa, her parents had disowned her. Papa wasn't grand enough for them. They had had a marquis in mind for Mama, not the son of a poor country parson.

My feeling was that if Papa wasn't good enough for them, then I wasn't good enough either. I knew that Colonel Lennox, Papa's commanding officer, had promised Papa that he would see I was safely united with my grandparents, so before he could put this delightful scheme into practice, I had decamped. My emotions had been rather in a muddle at the time, and it had seemed a good idea. Now I wasn't so sure.

I was eighteen years old. For how long could I realistically pretend to be a fifteen-year-old boy?

But if I told Mr. Fitzallan the truth, he would ship me off to my grandparents. And I still had very negative feelings about those two. They had never even written to Mama. Without ever having met them, I disliked them thoroughly.

Of course, if I refused to tell Mr. Fitzallen my true name, there was little likelihood of his being able to trace who I was. In effect, he would be stuck with me.

Unaccountably, my spirits lifted. Poor Mr. Fitzallan, I thought unrepentantly. And grinned.

I blew out the candle and settled down into my pillow. As I was drifting off to sleep, a very disturbing thought jarred my tranquility. Mr. Fitzallan did not own Carlton Castle. It was the Earl of Leyburn I would have to deal with. And that prospect was not so pleasant.

The earl arrived home the following week. The household had been expecting him for two days, and when his curricle appeared in the stable yard, there was a flurry of subdued activity. Mr. Fitzallan, who had been watching me work Saladin in the large paddock, moved instantly to greet his cousin.

"Diccon! How wonderful to have you back," he called.

I pulled the stallion up and looked curiously at the man swinging down from the carriage. He was very dark. I would have taken him for a Spaniard had I not known who he was. His hair was soot-black and worn longer than I was accustomed to see in the army. He looked as if he were deeply suntanned, although May was much too early in the year to account for that color. He was not as tall as Mr. Fitzallan and not as massively built. The two men stood for a moment in conversation and then began moving my way. I felt my heart begin to beat faster.

"Here is your new horse, Diccon," Mr. Fitzallan was saying. "He was delivered by the boy who is presently on his back."

Richard Fitzallan raised his head and looked at me. His eyes were as dark as his hair. He had the face of an archangel.

"So," he said coolly, "you are able to ride this hellion?"

"Yes, my lord," I stammered.

The earl's eyes narrowed. "And who are you?" he asked.

"My name is Valentine Brown, my lord," I said with some dignity.

Lord Leyburn's eyes held none of the gentleness of Mr. Fitzallan's. "Valentine Brown. Of course. That explains everything." He looked amused. "Well, go on, Valentine Brown. Let's see what you can do with him."

I looked questioningly at Mr. Fitzallan. "Go on, Valentine," he said quietly. "Just do as you were doing earlier."

I nodded and turned Saladin along the rail. We began to canter. After a few minutes I ventured to glance at Lord Leyburn. He was watching Saladin intently and after another minute he called to me to pull up.

"Thank you," he said to me. "I'll be along to ride him in the morning." Then he turned to Mr. Fitzallan. "Come up to the house with me, Ned. I could use a glass of wine."

Mr. Fitzallan smiled at his cousin affectionately. "You must tell me how everything went," he said.

The two men walked up the path to the castle.

I spent the rest of the day worrying about tomorrow morning. "I'll ride him," Lord Leyburn had said so casually. The question was, Would he?

I didn't know what to hope for, what to think. If he rode Saladin, there would be no more use for me. If he didn't, he might decide I was useless as well. After all, he had bought the stallion as a mount for himself, not for me.

I put no trust in the earl's compassion as I had in his cousin's. Those disturbingly dark eyes had looked very hard. He reminded me of someone, but I couldn't place who it was. It bothered me all evening, and then, just before I fell asleep, some lines of poetry popped into my head: "Created thing naught valu'd he nor shunn'd." It was a moment before I recognized the lines. They were from Milton's *Paradise Lost*. And then I knew who the Earl of Leyburn reminded me of.

He came down to the stable at nine the following morning accompanied by Mr. Fitzallan. I saddled Saladin and brought him out of the stable and over into the paddock where the men were waiting. Lord Leyburn was dressed in buckskin riding breeches, high, polished boots, and a single-breasted hunting jacket that fit beautifully and looked as if it had seen many seasons of wear.

The extraordinary dark eyes considered me for an unnerving moment and then he said, "Get up on him, please."

"Me?"

He didn't answer but stood regarding me impassively. I could feel my cheeks turn scarlet. I turned to Saladin. The stirrup was a long way from the ground, but I am athletic. I swung up into the saddle.

"Trot him around the paddock until you feel him loosening up."

"Yes, my lord." My cheeks were still hot as I turned Saladin along the rail.

When I brought him back, Lord Leyburn said calmly, "Now, get off." When I was standing in front of Saladin holding his reins, the earl came over to stand next to me. He was not as tall as his cousin, but he was over six feet. I felt unpleasantly small standing beside him. He began to talk to Saladin. The stallion's ears pricked forward.

After five minutes the earl reached out to pat the stallion and Saladin did not try to back away. The earl reached into his pocket for a carrot, which Saladin gobbled greedily.

"Hold him while I get on," the earl said to me, and he moved to the horse's left side.

He was on Saladin's back in a flash, and crossing over my stirrups, which were far too short, he nudged the horse along the fence.

Saladin was nervous with the strange weight on his back, and the earl let him move into a canter. They came by us once and he called to Mr. Fitzallan, "Open the gate, Ned!" The next time around they swept past us in full gallop, out of the paddock and toward the moors.

"Heavens," I said weakly.

Mr. Fitzallan grinned and put a hand on my shoulder. "Diccon rides like a centaur," he said. "Always has. He's going to love that stallion."

I took a deep breath. "Then I suppose that means my job here is over."

Ned Fitzallan's kind, handsome face looked concerned. "It might mean that," he said. "Lord Leyburn asked me about you. He is not inclined toward turning his home into a refuge for indigent runaways."

The words I recognized as Lord Leyburn's. Mr. Fitzallan would never have spoken in such a manner.

"I am not running away," I protested.

"Aren't you, Valentine?" He looked at me with ineffable kindness, and I swallowed a lump in my throat. "Well, you will just have to convince Lord Leyburn of that, won't you?" He gave my shoulder a sympathetic squeeze and walked away.

4

The inevitable interview with Lord Leyburn came at four o'clock that afternoon. I was helping some of the lads clean tack when Hutchins came to tell me I was wanted at the castle.

"And you had better have something to say for yourself, Valentine," he warned me. "His lordship can't abide a liar."

I raised my chin in what I hoped was a dignified gesture. "I am not a liar," I said grandly.

"You had better not be," he returned darkly, and with those ominous words ringing in my ears I walked up to the castle.

I scrubbed my hands and face, brushed my

hair until it shone, and changed my shirt before I went to find Crosby.

"His lordship wants to see me, I believe," I told the upright old man who was Lord Leyburn's butler.

"He does indeed, Valentine. He's in the library, and you're to go right along in to him. It's the first room down this hall."

I took a deep breath and squared my shoulders. Crosby put his hand to his face and coughed.

"It's not the hangman, lad," he said.

"I don't know about that," I mumbled glumly, and went off down the hall.

The library had to be the most comfortable room in the castle. It was medium-sized, book-lined, and the furniture was all well-worn leather and chinz. There was a fire burning in the huge stone fireplace and the earl was seated in a chair near it, his long booted legs stretched before him. Mr. Fitzallan was standing by the window looking serious. The dogs, who were curled up at the earl's feet, came over to greet me and then returned to their places. The dark head turned in my direction.

"You wished to see me, my lord?" I asked.

"Yes, I did. Come in, Valentine Brown."

I walked halfway across the room and stopped, facing him. I waited.

"I want to know why you are here," he said.

"I—I needed a job, my lord, and the Marquis of Rayleigh needed someone to deliver Saladin to you."

"And why did you need a job?" He had a clear, beautifully pitched voice, the sort of voice that commanded effortlessly. Without making a move or raising a hand, he was intimidating me.

"I needed the money," I said flatly.

"Because your father had died?"

"Yes, my lord."

"I believe you told Mr. Fitzallan that your father was an army officer who was killed in the recent retreat from Spain?"

"Yes, my lord."

"What was his commission?"

There was silence as I realized what I had just admitted. I had never told Mr. Fitzallan my father was an officer. I said nothing.

"I have little patience with these kinds of games, Valentine," Lord Leyburn said. "You will answer my question."

"No," I said. "I won't."

"I see." His voice had kept the same tone of pleasant command all through the interview. "Well, then, you had better pack your bag and leave. Mr. Fitzallan will give you whatever wages you have coming."

I felt as if the bottom had dropped out of my world. Until this minute I hadn't really believed

I would be sent away. I looked at Mr. Fitzallan.

"Diccon," that darling, sweet man protested. "You can't just run the boy out. Where will he go?"

"That's his lookout," his lordship returned. More than ever he was resembling Milton's Satan. Then he added, startlingly, "If he can't trust me, then I can't trust him."

"But I don't know you," I said.

He raised his eyebrows. The answer to that fatuous remark was so obvious that I found myself smiling. "I will tell you why I'm here," I said, "but I won't tell you my name."

Lord Leyburn waved me to a seat. "Well, that's a start, at least. All right, Valentine. Let's hear it."

I gave him the bare bones of my story, omitting the name and rank of my grandparents and omitting as well to mention that I had changed my gender when I ran away.

"Papa was quite convinced that my grandparents would take me in," I concluded, "and I suppose he was right. That was not the sort of thing he would leave to chance. But I don't want any part of them. I can manage on my own. As far as I'm concerned, they're nothing but a pair of scoundrels. Do you know, they never even *wrote* to my mother? Not once?"

"Valentine, my dear boy, that is very distressing, no doubt, but do please consider. Your father was most certainly in touch with your grandparents. They expect to take care of you. And it won't be long before you are old enough to be truly independent. Do please let us get in touch with them for you." It was Mr. Fitzallan, my only ally, and I stared at him reproachfully.

"I'd rather starve," I said—dramatically but as it happens, truthfully.

"So would I," said the Earl of Leyburn, and I looked at him in astonishment.

"You would?"

"Certainly." He rose to his feet in a single fluid movement.

"Diccon!"

His lordship smiled. He was beautiful when he was angry but when he smiled . . . I realized I wasn't breathing and took a gulp of air.

"Damn it all, Ned, you wouldn't send the lad to a cold-blooded pair like that, would you? Yes, I can see you would. Well, I won't. He can stay on here. We'll just have to make some arrangements."

"Diccon, you can't just appropriate a boy like this. The law won't allow it."

It was gradually being borne in on me that Mr. Fitzallan—kind, dear, sweet Mr. Fitzallan—had not dealt with me sooner because he had been counting on his lordship to do it for him.

"In this part of the world, I *am* the law." The

earl did not even sound arrogant when he said that. He was stating a fact. He looked at me and I blinked at the brilliant laughter in his eyes. "Christ, Valentine," he said, "but you can ride."

"I'm always needing someone to run errands for me," his lordship had said casually when he discussed my position in the house, and as the weeks of May and June went by, that is what I found myself doing to earn my keep. Most of the errands involved his lordship's tenants and dependents, who comprised nearly the whole northeastern section of Yorkshire, I discovered. In this part of the world, the Earl of Leyburn was indeed the law. But he was far more than that— he was protector, benefactor, and a source of tremendous local pride. In Yorkshire, the Earl of Leyburn ranked just slightly below God.

What I loved best, however, were the times he would take Saladin out on the moors and allow me to come along. He knew every stone of the Dales, every waterfall, every hill, every farmer and farmer's family. I loved the country. There was something about it—a wildness, a freshness —that went to my head and made me want to shout and laugh and run like a young colt, for the sheer pleasure of it.

I think Lord Leyburn sensed my response and was pleased by it, for as the weeks passed, he took me farther and farther afield, through all the wild, remote, and beautiful places of the Pennines.

The agricultural business in this part of Yorkshire was sheep. For centuries the farmers of the dales had been supplying wool to the weavers in Leeds and Bradford. The wool industry was beyond comparison the greatest source of wealth in Yorkshire, and the Fitzallan family had been fostering it since the Middle Ages—on the agricultural end only.

"I was in a factory in Leeds once," Lord Leyburn told me. A look of inexpressible distaste crossed his face. "A hellish place. No air. Noise. Not fit for human habitation. I couldn't wait to get out. I can't understand why anyone would want to leave the country and go to work in a place like that."

We were riding toward the Buttertubs Pass between Wensleydale and Swaledale, and the wild mountain scenery around us was truly magnificent. Lord Leyburn turned Saladin onto a steep narrow road and I followed on Cavalier, his lordship's big bay gelding.

"Someone has to make the cloth," I said mildly.

I could hear him grunt. "I suppose so. But at least they could put windows in the damned places. Bloody cits."

"Why don't you start a model factory?" I suggested.

Saladin stopped and the Earl of Leyburn turned to look at me. He didn't say anything, and I looked silently back at that magnificent face and grinned. With the greatest effort of imagination possible, I still couldn't picture him in a factory.

"Watch your footing here," he said. "The road runs right along the side of a deep gorge."

He started forward again and I followed, looking around me appreciatively. Buttertubs Pass was one of the highest mountain passes in England, Lord Leyburn had told me. It took its name from certain holes in the ground near its top, which were called Buttertubs because of their shape.

Near the summit of the pass Lord Leyburn pulled up once again and signaled to me to dismount. We tied the horses and stood for a minute looking about us.

"Look back toward Swaledale," he said, and obediently I followed his eyes. "The stream, or beck, at the bottom of the gorge there is called Cliff Beck," he told me. "It runs away down into Muker Beck and then to the Swale. That hill there"—he pointed—"is Great Shunnor Fell, and that one is Lovely Seat."

"Lovely Seat?" I echoed incredulously.

He grinned. There was a slight wind and it blew his black hair onto his forehead. He threw his head back a little. "The names are Norse. *Sjowar* means a lookout hill and Lovely Seat comes from *luin,* which means alarm. They were probably sentry lookouts in the old days."

His black hair was still falling over his brow, and I had a sudden, alarming urge to reach up and smooth it back for him. I put my hands in my pockets.

"Well, where are these famous Buttertubs?" My voice sounded strange and I cleared my throat.

"Over this way."

I stared, awestruck, down into the menacing pit that was sunk into the flat surface near the crest of the pass. The rock faces descending into the one-hundred-foot-deep depression were so beautifully fluted it did not seem possible they were the work of nature and not of man.

"It was done by rainwater eating away at the limestone," the earl said. He was standing right next to me. "Uncanny, isn't it?"

I felt breathless. "It certainly is." There was the sound of a curlew crying in the distance. I looked up but did not see it. The cry came again.

"What is that?" Lord Leyburn said sharply, and started toward the next depression. I followed.

"Christ." We both looked down into the frightful hole and saw the same thing: a child clinging to one of the narrow edges. The small face turned up to us looked absolutely terrified.

"Christ," the earl repeated, and then he turned to me. "I'll climb down there with him. He can't be left alone—he might try to climb out and fall. You ride into Thwaite, Valentine, and get help. We need men and some good strong rope. Try Hambleton at the feed store first."

He was taking off his coat as he spoke, and now he called to the boy on the ledge. "Hold on, lad! I'm coming down to you. No need to be afraid."

I stared in horror at the sheer rock face below me. I put my hand on his forearm. It was hard as the rock we were standing on.

"My lord," I said breathlessly, "you don't have to climb down. Wait until I get back with some rope."

He pulled away from me and lowered himself over the edge. As he disappeared into the pit, he looked up once, briefly, and grinned. "It won't be the first time I've done it," he said. "Now go."

I went. I took Saladin and rode as hard as I could down the other side of the pass toward the village of Thwaite. And the whole terrible way my mind was filled with visions of that strong, arrogant, splendid body crumpled and broken at the bottom of the Buttertubs.

5

I had never been in Thwaite before, but it was a typical Dales village and I galloped into the main street over the small humpbacked bridge and spotted the store his lordship had mentioned almost immediately.

The proprietor, Mr. Hambleton, moved promptly enough to carry out Lord Leyburn's orders, but he did not appear unduly concerned about the situation. He collected two other men from the town and they hung some lengths of good stout rope over their saddles.

"Hurry, can't you?" I burst out at one point.

Mr. Hambleton gave me a surprised look. Then he patted my shoulder. "We've moving as fast as we can, lad, but there's naught to worry about. His lordship is there."

"If he didn't fall himself," I said with anguish, and the horrible picture flashed through my mind again.

"Fall? His lordship?" Mr. Hambleton looked astonished. "He won't fall, lad," he said reassuringly. "And he'll have the child well in hand, believe me. You'll see."

I heard before I saw. We were still a little distance from the top of the pass when we heard a clear, resonant voice vigorously declaiming a very funny and extremely vulgar song.

Mr. Hambleton turned to me with a grin. "There, lad, didn't I tell you?"

We dismounted and went to peer over the rim of the pit. There, below us, seated side by side on the ledge, their legs dangling over an eighty-foot drop, sat the Earl of Leyburn and a small boy. The earl was singing lustily and the boy was convulsed with giggles.

"Well, now, my lord," Mr. Hambleton called placidly, "what do you want us to do?"

His lordship looked up at us. He appeared to be enjoying himself enormously. "How are you, Archie?" he called back.

"Fine, my lord, thank you."

"If you would throw some rope down here, perhaps you and the others could pull this young cawker up. Who is that you've got with you?"

"It's us, my lord," said Mr. Hambleton's two companions, and they came to peer over the edge of the Buttertubs.

"How are you, Will? Dan, how's the wife?" his lordship asked amiably. He might have been at a social gathering.

"Better, my lord, thank you. She enjoyed the fruit you sent."

"Are you ready, my lord?" asked Mr. Hambleton.

"Send it down," said the earl.

The rope was duly tossed down and Lord Leyburn secured it under the armpits of the child.

"After we pull the boy up, we'll send the rope back down for you, my lord," Archie Hambleton said, and then the three men began to draw the child up to safety. When his feet touched the ground at the top of the pit, the boy began to cry. He was quite small; I didn't think he was more than seven years old.

"It's all right, sweetheart," I said softly. "You're perfectly safe now. Let me take that rope off you."

Still crying, the boy lifted his arms and I began to undo the knot.

"Now, my lord, I said we'd send the rope for you," said Archie Hambleton's voice resignedly, and I turned to see a familiar black head rising over the top of the pit.

"You might have slipped," said Will.

Lord Leyburn's dark eyes were brilliant in the sunlight. I knew suddenly, with absolute certainty, that it was the danger he had enjoyed more than the climb.

"Well, I didn't," he said, and turned his attention to the boy. "What is this, Frank? Crying?"

"N-no, my lord," the boy said, tears streaming down his face.

"No need to cry," his lordship said briskly. "If you do, you'll frighten my horse and then how will you ride with me?"

"R-ride with you, my lord?" The tears stopped and the child's eyes enlarged noticeably.

"Certainly. I'm going to take you home myself. But first . . ." His lordship removed his handkerchief and did a very efficient mopping-up job on Frank's grimy, wet face.

"Perhaps you ought to take Cavalier," I murmured. "Saladin just had a rather vigorous run to the village."

His lordship looked amused. "I didn't tell you to take Saladin."

"He was faster."

"Yes, well, I'm afraid that means Frank is going to have to settle for Cavalier. You take Saladin on home, Valentine."

"Yes, my lord." I watched as he lifted the boy into the saddle and turned to speak to the men who had come to the rescue. Then I mounted

Saladin and turned down the pass toward Hardraw and home.

Mr. Fitzallan was in the stable yard when I came in riding Saladin, and I had to tell him the story of our adventure.

"If that isn't just like Diccon," he said with half-exasperated affection. "He could have entertained the child just as well from the top of the pit, but he wanted the risk of the climb."

"He wouldn't have been able to reassure the boy half so well from above," I said. "The poor child was in a panic."

"Perhaps. But he wouldn't have moved if Diccon had kept talking to him."

This was indisputably true, as was the other half of Mr. Fitzallan's original statement. His lordship had wanted the climb.

"Come along back to the house with me, Valentine," Mr. Fitzallan said, changing the subject. "I want to talk to you."

He sounded very grave, and my heart sank. "Yes, sir," I said obediently, and walked beside him up the drive toward the castle.

We went into the library and he gestured to me to sit down on the old leather sofa. I loved this room. I had been in it a few times since my initial interview with the earl and I looked now at the two dogs comfortably curled near the hearth and snapped my fingers. The big sheep dog came to me immediately and I bent to scratch his ears. The collie stayed where he was. He went to no one but Lord Leyburn.

"The time has come, Valentine, to do something about regularizing your position," Mr. Fitzallan said.

"Sir?"

"His lordship may think it is all very well to have you spend your days trailing around at his heels, but the fact remains that you are not a servant. In the normal course of events you would be at school."

My mouth dropped open. "School?"

"I presume you have heard of school." His voice held not a trace of sarcasm.

"Of course," I said hastily. "But I'm afraid my education has been rather sketchy, sir. I was never sent to school. I had a—a tutor." In point of fact, my mother had taught me how to read and write and do my sums, and my father had taught me history. Papa had been devoted to history and I had caught his enthusiasm.

"I see. And what profession had you planned to follow, Valentine? The army?"

I looked at him blankly. "The army, sir?"

"Valentine." He sounded very patient. "Surely your father discussed your future with you. What were his plans? What did he intend you to do with yourself in life?"

Papa had presumed I would marry, of course,

but I could hardly say that to Mr. Fitzallan. Marriage was not considered a career for a boy.

"I beg your pardon, sir. I'm being very stupid. Of course I planned to follow Papa into the army. We didn't discuss it very much, you see. I always just assumed that is what I would do."

That's better, I approved myself. That sounds reasonable.

"And do you still desire a commission?"

"Yes, sir."

"A commission costs a great deal of money."

I bit my lip and stared at the pattern on the faded Persian rug. "Well," I said uncomfortably, "I know I won't be able to get a commission now."

The door opened and the Earl of Leyburn walked into the room. I looked at his dark angel's face and felt a surge of happiness so intense it was like pain. He glanced at me and then turned to his cousin.

"Am I interrupting you, Ned?" He bent to bestow a brief caress on the collie, who had immediately come over to greet him.

"Valentine and I have been discussing his future," Mr. Fitzallan said calmly. "He really cannot go on as he has been doing, Diccon. Surely you can see that."

"Why not?" said his lordship, and sat down in his favorite chair. The sheep dog immediately deserted me and went to lie at his feet. "Are you unhappy, Valentine?"

"No, my lord," I said fervently.

"Then, what is the difficulty, Ned?" His dark eyes looked enigmatic as they rested on his cousin's face.

"Diccon, it must be as clear to you as it is to me that Valentine's future does not lie at Carlton Castle. And it is his future we must be concerned for. He is too young to think of it for himself."

Mr. Fitzallan meant every word he said. His kind heart was truly concerned for me. He wanted to plan my life for me, set me on the path of self-sufficiency and prosperity. I heartily wished he would keep quiet.

His lordship's finely modeled dark head turned my way. "And what do you desire to do with your life, Valentine?"

"I want to stay here with you," I answered promptly.

A slow smile lit his eyes and pulled at the corners of his mouth.

"Why not?" he said.

"For God's sake, Diccon . . ." Mr. Fitzallan began, and Lord Leyburn's eyes narrowed.

"That's enough, Ned." His lordship's voice had lost its pleasantness and there was the distinct spark of temper in his eyes. "*I* will decide what is to be done with Valentine," he said, and the edge of the temper was in his voice as well. "It is not a subject you need concern yourself with."

The room was very quiet. There was a tight look around Mr. Fitzallan's mouth. The two men looked at each other and then Mr. Fitzallan said, "Very well, Diccon."

The austere look on his lordship's face relaxed. He nodded.

Mr. Fitzallan stood up. "If you'll excuse me," he said, "I have an appointment with Mowbray."

"Of course, Ned," the earl said courteously. Mr. Fitzallan left the room and Lord Leyburn turned to me. "Well, brat," he said. "What have you to say for yourself?"

I felt sorry for Mr. Fitzallan, but I wasn't fool enough to say that now. "I like it here," I told him. "I don't want to leave."

"Well, I don't want you to leave. So that is that." He stretched and yawned. "Hand me the newspaper, will you, Valentine?"

I leapt to oblige him and put the paper into his outstretched hand. That hand fascinated me—the hard power of it, the beauty. He opened the paper and began to read. My eyes moved from his hand to his absorbed face.

I was looking, I thought, at the last of the great feudal lords. For Lord Leyburn was that—in temperament if not in fact. He ruled here at

Carlton Castle as if he were a prince, had done so ever since he had become the earl at the age of sixteen. From boyhood on up he had done as he pleased with never anyone to say him nay. He wouldn't care if the king himself were after me, I thought. If he wanted me to stay, then stay I would.

I rose to my feet and silently slipped from the room. He didn't appear to notice my leaving.

6

"What do you think, Val?"

I came back to reality with a start and tried to focus my attention. "I beg your pardon?"

"I said what do you think Sim should do?" I must have continued to look blank, for Georgie, the redhaired groom who was addressing me, looked suddenly exasperated. "Haven't you been listening to me?"

I had not. We were in the tack room idly rolling dice, and my mind had not been on what Georgie was saying at all.

"I'm sorry," I said quickly. "My wits were wandering. What did you ask me?"

"It's about Sim," Georgie repeated patiently.

"He has a chance to get a farm over by Scarborough. His uncle wants him to come help work it, and then, when the uncle dies, it will be his. Do you think he should do it?"

"What does Sim want to do?" I asked.

"He wants to go. But his mother is against it. There won't be any wages on the farm, see, and he gives her what he gets here."

I nodded. "But, Georgie, what can I do? It's Sim's decision, surely."

Georgie's freckled face looked unhappy. "He's afraid of his mother, Val. He should take it. It's a chance for independence for him. But he won't listen to me." Georgie picked up the dice and shook them absentmindedly. "He'll listen to you," he said.

This was not the first time I had found myself in this sort of position, and it troubled me. I didn't understand why these boys with whom I had made friends should turn to me for solutions to their problems.

"Does his mother need his wages?" I asked.

"No. Sim's the youngest and she lives with his older brother on the farm that was Sim's father's. They're Lord Leyburn's tenants, so you know they want for nothing."

"Then Sim should accept his uncle's offer," I said.

"Will you tell him that, Val?"

I knew from Georgie's face that this was important. It was Sim's whole future that was in question. I nodded. "I'll talk to him."

Georgie grinned. "Good."

I looked at him in puzzlement. "But, Georgie, why should Sim listen to me more than to you? I'm younger than you both."

"That doesn't matter," he answered. Then he frowned. "You aren't like us, Val."

"Because I speak differently?"

"No." Georgie stopped jiggling the dice and looked at me curiously. "You're not afraid of anything, Val, are you?"

I was so surprised I couldn't answer him.

Lord Leyburn had to go into Harrogate for the day and he had left a message for me to ride by the Slaters' farm to see how young Frank had recovered from his adventure with the Buttertubs. After my conversation with Georgie, I saddled Cavalier and rode off to do my errand.

The Slaters' farm stretched away over the high moors near Oughtershaw, a piece of starkest Yorkshire. Scattered over the miles upon bare miles of bare hillside were the stone barns I had grown accustomed to seeing all over Yorkshire and the Slater farmhouse was made of the same material.

I had a cozy tea with Mrs. Slater and Frank and

rode back home in the sunshine, sniffing the sharp sweetness of the air.

The problem of my future, a problem I had been ignoring determinedly for quite some time now, kept pushing through to the surface of my mind. Lord Leyburn had said I could stay at Carlton Castle, but Lord Leyburn thought I was a boy. What would he say when he found out the truth? I thought of the temper that had flared in his face when Mr. Fitzallan had tried to cross him. How would he feel when he discovered that I had deceived him?

Georgie thought I was afraid of nothing. Georgie was wrong.

I met Lord Leyburn returning from Harrogate when I was two miles away from the castle. He greeted me with a smile, and our two horses began to walk side by side along the roadway. His lordship had not spoken after his initial greeting and I stole a glance at him out of the corner of my eye. He was frowning a little.

"Are you still in the attic room?" he asked me abruptly.

"Why, yes, my lord." The question had taken me completely by surprise.

"You shouldn't be." His face looked very severe. "Ned was right about one thing. You aren't a servant."

"I like my room," I said. "I don't want to change it."

He gave me a strange, slanting look. "What do you want to change?" he asked. "What do you miss from your old life?"

I answered before I thought. "Music."

He stopped his horse. He was not riding Saladin today but a very well-bred-looking chestnut mare. "Do you play?" he asked.

"Yes. Piano, not harpsichord. My mother was a very fine musician and she gave me lessons when I was a child. But I've had few opportunities for formal study since then. We always had a piano, though. Papa saw to that for me."

I stopped speaking suddenly. Surely this sounded like an odd background for a boy. Girls were the ones who were encouraged to play an instrument.

Lord Leyburn said nothing, however, and began to walk his horse forward again. He did not speak until we were in the stable yard and then only to say, "Come up to the house with me."

I obeyed without comment, stretching my legs to try to keep up with his long stride, concentrating on keeping my face serene. What was he going to do?

He took me into the drawing room. It was an enormous chamber that had been the banqueting hall of the old castle. It was stiff and formal, and even on this sunny July day, it was cold and damp. On the far side of the room, near the fireplace, was a piano. Lord Leyburn gestured.

"Try it," he said.

I moved slowly across the marble floor, sat down on the bench, and ran my fingers along the keyboard. In this cold and damp and unused room, the piano was in perfect tune. I looked up at the earl.

"Go on," he said quietly.

I played Mozart's "Sonata in C Major," which I had always liked and which was not too difficult. It was a beautiful piano. When I finished I stayed as I was, my eyes on the keyboard.

"You play with a great deal of feeling," said his lordship.

I forced a smile. "What you really mean is that my technique is terrible."

"No. I don't mean that at all. You need more work, true, but technique can be learned. What you have is something that can't be taught."

I looked up at him. His face was as serious as mine.

"What is that?" I asked.

"It is hard to put it into words. It's an understanding, but it's an emotion as well."

I nodded. "Do you play, my lord?"

"Yes." Just that single word, with no qualifiers and no disclaimers. He played.

"What would you like to hear?" he asked.

I got up from the piano. "Haydn's 'Sonata Number Five in C Major?' " I asked tentatively. It was a piece whose difficulty was about on the level of the Mozart I had just played. He smiled very faintly and sat down in my vacated place.

I knew at once why the piano was in such perfect tune. He played as he did everything else: with the brilliance that was an integral part of his nature. There was passion in his music and the knowledge of suffering and of joy. His playing wasn't even remotely amateur; his technique was flawless.

When he finished, I stared for a minute at the long hard fingers on the keys.

"Well?" His face was inscrutable.

There was no need to tell him how well he played. He knew that already. "Please," I asked softly, "would you play some more?"

Without another word he turned back to the keyboard. I sat down on the edge of an extremely uncomfortable chair and for another hour felt myself in heaven.

When finally I went upstairs to my room, it was to find Robert, one of the footmen, engaged in putting together my clothes.

"What are you doing?" I asked sharply.

"His lordship wants you moved to the blue bedroom downstairs," he told me.

"What?" I sat down on my familiar sagging bed and gaped at him.

"Mr. Crosby gave me orders to move your things to the blue bedroom," Robert said woodenly. "You're coming up in the world, Val. Or should I say Master Valentine?"

"Stow it, Robert," I said inelegantly, and after a minute he grinned.

"Well, like it or not, Val, you're moving." Robert looked eloquently at the shabby jacket he was holding. "You'll be getting new clothes next, I expect. Perhaps his lordship is planning to adopt you."

"I'm not a candidate for adoption," I said fiercely. I, too, stared at the jacket. God, what was I going to do if I had to be measured for new clothes?

I picked up the book that was on the floor next to my bed and glumly followed Robert down the stairs to the part of the house the family used. I had not been in the bedroom wing before, and when Robert pushed open a door, I stared in wonder at the big, sunny, comfortable room. Army quarters had never looked like this.

"However can we have the card game here?" I asked suddenly. Robert and John and Mickey, three of the footmen, had taught me to play a very complicated game of cards and we had taken to meeting a few nights a week in my old room.

"Will you still want to play with us?" Robert's voice sounded muffled, and I stared at him.

"Of course I want to play. How else am I to get my spending money?" I had been very successful at that card game.

Robert laughed. "We'll have to find another spot. If Mr. Crosby ever found out, we'd be in trouble. He hates gambling."

We played for pennies, hardly a princely sum, and no one was ever financially hurt by the games. But Crosby was a little unreasonable on the subject of cards. We had only begun to play when I offered my room. No one else had the luxury of privacy.

After Robert left, I walked slowly around the room, touching the surfaces of polished wood, picking up the fine china ornaments. Finally I came to a halt in front of the great mahogany-framed mirror.

I had not seen myself in a full-length mirror since I had come to Carlton Castle. My old room had held a little bit of glass for shaving, only large enough to make sure that my face was clean. I stood now and stared at myself critically. When Lord Leyburn looked at me, what did he see?

The slight figure looking back at me was straight and lithe as a boy's, the legs long, the hips slim. I needed a haircut badly. At present I looked rather like an untidy page boy. I stepped a little closer to the mirror and stared appraisingly at my face.

The eyes that looked back at me were large and dark, more gray than blue; the long dark lashes looked betrayingly feminine, as did the finely textured skin. However, the face itself was thin, not full, and that helped to give an illusion of boyishness. The mouth and chin were finely modeled and firm, not soft. I looked like what his lordship thought I was: a delicately-featured fifteen-year-old boy.

But if I had to be measured for clothes . . . my disguise would not hold up under that kind of a scrutiny.

In a sense it would be a relief to be found out. If I could only be certain that I would be allowed to continue as I was, I would tell Lord Leyburn the truth myself. For some obscure reason, I had begun to want him to see me as a girl. I stared at my masculine reflection and wondered what Lord Leyburn would think if he ever saw me in a gown. After a minute I turned away from the mirror in exasperation. I must, I thought wryly, be going out of my mind.

7

The day following my move into the family wing I arrived in the kitchen as usual for breakfast. Mrs. Scone looked at me doubtfully. "I was going to send Robert to your room with a tray, Valentine. I don't think it proper for you to be eating in the kitchen anymore."

The last thing I needed was Robert darting in and out of my bedroom. "I have every intention of continuing to eat in the kitchen," I said. "I hate to eat alone, and besides, I like you all very much. It's fun eating here. Did you make muffins this morning, Mrs. Scone?"

Mrs. Scone laughed and ruffled my hair. "What a boy you are, Valentine. Yes, I made muffins. Sit you down and I'll get you a plate."

Later that morning, as I was lunging a yearling for Hutchins, I looked toward the fence and saw his lordship there watching me. When I had finished with the youngster, I made a fuss over him and gave him an apple.

"You have a magic touch with horses, Valentine," said a voice at my shoulder, and I smiled a little.

"They're very sensitive creatures, my lord. They know who loves them." As if to prove my point, the youngster began to nuzzle Lord Leyburn's chest. He laughed.

"So they do. I want you to come along with me this afternoon, Valentine." He signaled to Georgie, who came over to take the yearling.

I grinned at Georgie and began to walk after the earl. "Where are we going?"

"To Middleham." He didn't say anything more and kept his silence all during the ride. I had never been to Middleham, even though it was not that far from Carlton and was the chief town of Coverdale. We went not to the town, however, but to the huge ruined castle that stands above it.

Still in silence, Lord Leyburn dismounted and I followed suit. He began to walk toward the great stone walls and I walked beside him, made uneasy by the still somberness of his face.

The great medieval ruin was eerily impressive, with its shattered battlements and roofless chambers where the birds had built their nests. I thought of Carlton, which might have looked like this if the family had deserted it, and shivered a little.

"Whose castle is this?" I asked softly.

"Richard's," the earl said gravely. Then as if he sensed my confusion, he looked down at me. "The last owner of this castle was Richard Plantagenet, King Richard the Third." He was not smiling.

"Oh." I looked around me. "It must have been very grand once."

"It was. The jewel of the north Middleham used to be. The Tudors let it fall into ruin."

I remembered what Mr. Fitzallan had told me about Richard III. "I understand that here in the north people do not think of King Richard as they do elsewhere," I said tentatively.

The earl's dark eyes were hard on my face. "No, they don't. Richard the Third, Valentine, is the most bitterly wronged king in all of English history."

I held his gaze. "I only know about him from Shakespeare."

His mouth twisted. "You and everyone else. Crookback Richard, villain, usurper, murderer. And none of it is true."

"What was Shakespeare's source?" I asked. One thing I had learned from my father was to evaluate the bias of historical sources before coming to any conclusions.

Lord Leyburn looked at me speculatively. "The *History of Richard III* by Sir Thomas More."

"Sir Thomas More?" I shook my head. "I don't think one can call into question the integrity of a man like More, my lord."

The earl made an abrupt gesture. "Sit down, Valentine." I sat on a low stone wall and stretched out my legs. Lord Leyburn did the same.

"Thomas More was brought up in the household of Cardinal Morton, the Archbishop of Canterbury. Morton was the right hand man of Henry the Seventh, the Tudor usurper who defeated Richard at Bosworth Field. Morton was also, and had been for years, Richard's deadly enemy. There is no doubt that Morton is the one who supplied the information about Richard to his pupil, Thomas More. And the history was never published in More's lifetime. It was found with his papers after his death. It was not finished. I've always thought that More, who was an extremely intelligent man, never finished it because he had begun to doubt the honesty and the value of the material supplied to him by Morton."

This was all extremely interesting. "Are there no other sources?" I asked thoughtfully.

"Nothing chronological. There are, of course, Parliamentary records and decrees, personal letters from the time, the Patent Rolls, things like that."

"Things like that can be very informative."

He was sitting a little distance from me, staring straight ahead at the town clustered on the next hill. His hands were lightly clenched on a leather riding crop, and the breeze from the moors lightly stirred the raven thickness of his hair.

"Very informative indeed, to those who care to look with an unbiased eye," he said, and his dark eyes turned to me. "What do you know of Richard the Third, Valentine?"

"That he murdered his nephews, the little princes in the tower," I answered promptly.

"And why would he do that, do you think? Richard had already been crowned king and widely accepted by the country."

"Because the princes were the sons of Edward the Fourth and Richard was only the former king's younger brother. They had a better right to the throne than he."

"So did the boy's five sisters. And his brother George's son and daughter. In getting rid of the boys he would only be scratching the surface of the York heirs who supposedly stood between him and the throne."

I narrowed my eyes and stared at the stone

walls of the ruined castle. "What happened to the other heirs?" I asked finally.

"You have a beautiful mind, Valentine," he said. "When Richard died, they were all alive and prospering."

"When Richard died," I repeated. "What happened to them after he died?"

"Henry took immediate steps to secure the persons of all of the heirs and kept them in close seclusion until he could get rid of them with a minimum of fuss."

"My, my, my." I looked at him. "No one ever claimed Henry the Seventh was a pleasant man," I remarked.

"He was more than unpleasant. He was the murdering bastard who had the princes killed," the earl said, and proceeded to set forth the evidence.

"But these are *facts*," I said when he had finished. "What you have just told me is there, in black and white, in the records of the time. Why has no one made this known?"

"Because most historians look only for what they want to find, not for what is there."

"I think it is outrageous," I said indignantly.

A little of the grimness softened from his face. "Ned thinks it's mad to get worked up over someone who has been dead four hundred years."

"The truth is never mad." I had learned that from my father. "And injustice, no matter how old it might be, is never tolerable. Why, they've stolen his good name."

He looked at me, and his face was transformed by a sudden blazing smile. "A beautiful mind," he repeated. "You're a lad after my own heart, Valentine."

For some reason I could not fathom I found myself having difficulty breathing. I could not tear my eyes away from his face. It was very quiet here at the castle now that our voices had ceased. I could hear the stillness. Then Lord Leyburn rose to his feet.

"Come," he said. "I don't like to leave the horses unattended for too long."

Mr. Fitzallan was riding ahead of us toward Carlton as we turned from the road onto the castle grounds, and his lordship shouted to him. There was enough room for three horses to ride abreast and Mr. Fitzallan waited until we came up to him before he began walking forward again, both of us flanking his lordship. The two men began to talk of some estate matter and I let my attention wander from their words, concentrating instead on their mood. There seemed to be perfect ease and amiability between them. No trace remained of the tension that had flared earlier over the subject of my future.

His lordship was nodding gravely. "Have Ellis come to see me," he said to his cousin. "I'll see to it."

Mr. Fitzallan smiled. "I already told him that."

The earl grinned and started to answer when his eye was caught by a strange carriage reposing in his stable yard. Georgie and Sim were in the process of unharnessing a pair of very smart-looking chestnuts.

"Cartington," Lord Leyburn said, "this is a surprise."

"Is it?" Mr. Fitzallan looked ironic. "You have to fish or cut bait on this one, Diccon. The duke isn't going to stand for any delay."

The earl said something I hadn't heard since army days in Ireland and his cousin chuckled. "Tell that to his grace," he suggested.

At that Lord Leyburn laughed. "Perhaps I will," he said, and turned Cavalier toward the path that led from the stable yard up to the house.

8

I sat on Magic Moment and watched Lord Leyburn's back for as long as it was visible. The Duke of Cartington. Here. When the earl was out of sight, I turned to find Mr. Fitzallan watching me curiously.

"Why do you look like that, Valentine?" he asked.

I stared at him, wide-eyed. "I'm not precisely accustomed to having dukes come to call," I said. "And the Duke of Cartington! That's a name almost as famous as the Earl of Leyburn's."

He looked amused. "Diccon would be pleased with that 'almost.' And yes, between them the Fitzallans and the Bevils ruled the north for

72

centuries. The present duke is a more powerful man than Diccon, however, as the Bevils never withdrew from government as did my family. But Diccon is still quite a prize and the duke would not be at all loath to capture him."

"A prize?" I asked in puzzlement. We had both dismounted by now and I looked up at him, squinting my eyes a little against the sun. He was really the most enormous man.

"A marriage prize," he explained with perfect and natural kindness. "The duke has a daughter and there has been talk of a match between Diccon and Lady Barbara."

I felt the bottom drop out of my stomach. I couldn't find the power to say a word.

"Actually, it would be a very good match for Diccon as well," Mr. Fitzallan was going on. His voice sounded a little strained. "The Fitzallans have always made dynastic marriages. Diccon's mother was the daughter of the Scots Duke of Oxnam." He smiled a little wryly. "Dukes seem to be running in the family of late. And Diccon's twenty-seven. It's time he married."

"Does—does he love Lady Barbara?" I asked faintly.

"Who knows, with Diccon? But that wouldn't necessarily weigh with him. Diccon is fully conscious of his duty to his name. And Lady Barbara is extremely beautiful." Uncharacteristically, he ran his hand through his hair. "She would have to be that," he said. "Diccon is not so dutiful that he'd marry a plain woman."

I looked at the tops of my boots. "Well, one can understand that. After all, he is so very beautiful himself."

"I know."

Mr. Fitzallan sounded rather grim and I raised my eyes to his face. "I sometimes think Diccon has been too blessed by the gods," he said. "He's spoiled. He has too much, he does everything too well. A little setback would be good for him."

"He's a very good landlord and patron." I felt somehow I had to stand up for the earl.

"Unquestionably. And he's an excellent high sheriff and justice of the peace. There isn't a county in England better run than this one is. He is always accessible and he is always just."

I kept my eyes on his face and remembered the discussion over my future. "But he doesn't like to be crossed."

"He never is, not since his father died." Mr. Fitzallan looked rueful. "I'm no match for him."

I saw his lordship's face in my mind and felt a pain squeeze at my heart. "Who is?" I asked very softly.

"I don't know. I'm afraid it's not Lady Barbara. If he wants her, she'll marry him. That's why the duke is here."

Mr. Fitzallan looked as unhappy as I felt. I took

his horse's reins and led both horses toward the stable.

The Duke of Cartington stayed for two days, and during that time I saw very little of Lord Leyburn. He spent most of his time with the duke, out on horseback or with a gun. I spent my time in the stable.

For some unaccountable reason, I was feeling very melancholy and lonely. Never before had the evils of my situation seemed so insurmountable. And yet I could not wish I had followed another course. I had never been one for regrets.

The Duke of Cartington left, and the day after his departure Lord Leyburn went into York for a few days. For centuries the Fitzallans had maintained a house in York, so Mr. Fitzallan informed me, and in York the Earl of Leyburn counted for rather more than the king.

I continued to feel restless and melancholy, and gravitated to the piano as if only music could release me from the oppressive mood that I could not account for. It was the first time in too long that I had had access to a piano, and with the duke gone, I took full advantage of it.

The earl's absence stretched from a few days to a week. Without him the house seemed strangely empty, as if all its vitality had been drained from it. Even the flowers in the garden seemed less brilliantly colored.

I was sitting at the piano picking out a melody in counterpoint, over and over again, when there came through the open windows the sound of voices on the drive. I went to the window and looked down.

Lord Leyburn was back. He was seated on the high seat of his phaeton, effortlessly holding his high-spirited pair at rest and looking down at Mr. Fitzallan, who stood on the drive beside him. He was laughing. As I watched, Robert went to the horses' heads, and his lordship, in a beautiful, fluid movement, swung himself down to the ground. He glanced up at the house, unaware of my presence. He was hatless and his thick black hair was tousled from the drive. His dark face looked fiercely beautiful in the clear sunlight. And it was then that I knew.

He had disappeared into the house and Jamie was bringing in his portmanteau before I stirred from the window. Oh no, I kept thinking over and over again, oh no, oh no, oh no.

I moved on leaden feet toward the piano bench, but before I reached it, his lordship appeared in the doorway.

"Valentine!" He gave me a smile. "I understand from Ned that you've been playing the keys off the piano."

I didn't know if I would be able to talk. I moved my lips and sound came out. "Yes, my lord."

He went toward the instrument himself, as if drawn by a magnet, and lightly ran his fingers over the keyboard. He looked up.

"There's to be a concert in York next week. I'll take you."

I could not look into his eyes and focused instead on his cravat. "Thank you, my lord." To my astonishment my voice sounded perfectly normal.

Crosby appeared in the doorway. "My lord," he said formally, "there is a message for you from his grace of Cartington. I put it on your desk in the library."

A flash of some emotion I couldn't identify went across his lordship's face, and then he nodded, said, "Thank you, Crosby," and left the room with his characteristic swift grace. I fled up the stairs to my room.

I understood at last why I had been so distressed by the news that Lord Leyburn was thinking of marriage. I understood at last the nature of my own feelings for him.

There had been between us, almost from the first, an affinity that I had known with no one else. My boyish guise had allowed us to learn about each other with no physical awareness to get in our way.

But now all that was changed—or at least it was changed for me. There was still that sense of spiritual affinity, but the physical was there as well. It was there in the darkness of his eyes, the fine modeling of his head, the strong slender sinews of his hands, the shape of his mouth.

God help me, I was in love with the Earl of Leyburn. And he thought I was a boy.

It would have been funny if it had not been so painful.

It was a pain that would get worse with every passing day. It was pain that I felt when I heard the sound of his voice, when I caught sight of his tall, lean figure, heard the sound of his footsteps coming up behind me.

I was terrified that I would betray myself. I could keep my face expressionless, my voice steady, but I could not keep myself from feeling. And the earl was intuitive. He was able to sense things that someone like Mr. Fitzallan, who operated solely on good sense and logic, would never apprehend. I supposed it was why his lordship was so marvelous with animals. But it was a danger to me; I knew it was. I was petrified he would sense the change in me. It wasn't a logical fear, but then the earl wasn't always logical. He was worse than logical. He was accurate.

I could, of course, tell him the truth. I thought of the scene, of his face when he discovered how I had deceived him. I thought of how his temper had flared at Mr. Fitzallan, and I prayed to God he would never look thus at me.

It was an impossible situation. My only comfort was the thought that the only person being hurt by it was myself.

9

"When we go into York," his lordship said to me the day after he arrived home, "we'll have to see about getting you some decent clothes. It should have been done long ago, as Ned pointed out to me last night." He smiled a little ruefully. "I'm afraid I'm not always as observant as I should be, lad."

Mr. Fitzallan came in on the end of this remark. "The problem, Diccon, is that most of your clothes are as old and as worn as Valentine's."

The earl grinned. "True enough."

"And if you are going to go up to London, you need some clothes, too," Mr. Fitzallan went on relentlessly.

"Ah." A black eyebrow was very slightly raised. "But I don't know yet if I am going up to London."

Mr. Fitzallan looked as if he would like to say something further but hadn't the nerve.

"Just so," his lordship said with amusement.

"There is a pile of papers on your desk that needs your attention," his cousin said stoically.

The earl looked suddenly alert. "The court papers I wanted prepared?"

"Yes."

"Good. I'll look at them now."

When he left, I looked up at Mr. Fitzallen. "Why will his lordship be going to London?" I asked.

"Lady Barbara is there for the Season. When Diccon didn't make an immediate offer, the duke decided to let her make her come-out. She is only eighteen. And very lovely. And an heiress. Diccon is a fool if he lets her get away."

I tried to speak lightly. "Surely there are other beautiful young heiresses in England."

"She is a Bevil, Valentine. From Northumberland. It would be a union of the two greatest families in the north."

It seemed that when it came to marriage alliances, Mr. Fitzallan was every bit as feudal as his ancestors. "I see," I said a little hollowly. Then, more aggressively, "If she is such a splendid match, why don't *you* marry her?"

There was an audible note of bitterness in his voice as he replied. "I am Diccon's cousin, Valentine, but I am not the earl. Lady Barbara Bevil is not for the likes of me."

It struck me suddenly that Mr. Fitzallan was not himself indifferent to the earl's prospective bride. I had blundered and hurt him. I put my hand on his arm and said, "Any girl would be lucky to marry you, sir."

And I meant it. I looked at his handsome face and thought how secure one would be married to a man like this. He was so kind, so considerate, so reliable. I thought of the man I loved and sighed. Next to his lordship, Mr. Fitzallen was stodgy and dull. How could I expect Lady Barbara to feel any differently? How could any girl not want to marry the Earl of Leyburn?

Later in the day I slipped out of the castle and went for a long walk on the moors.

I was finished. New clothing meant a tailor. I would have to tell the earl the truth. He would be angry, of course, but it couldn't make that big a difference to him. I was still the same person, wasn't I?

It was a very warm day and my jacket soon felt much too hot. I took it off, rolled up my sleeves, and walked on through the empty rolling miles of browns and greens and yellows. I was feeling strangely tired and lethargic and my legs felt heavy. Finally I threw myself down on the grass, put my hands behind my head, and stared up the high white clouds above me. What to do? What to do?

What I did was fall asleep, for the next thing I knew was the reverberation of horses hooves drumming on the ground. I sat up, a little bewildered. I saw Lord Leyburn at about the same time he saw me, for he slowed Saladin down and swung him in a wide arc around me.

"I didn't see you lying there in the grass," he said to me as he brought the stallion to a halt beside me.

His lordship dismounted, efficiently picketed Saladin, and dropped down beside me.

"What a day, eh," he said good-humoredly.

He was wearing buckskins and his favorite riding jacket, which he proceeded to take off. "It's hot as hell in this sun," he remarked, and started to roll up his sleeves. Belatedly I recalled my own state of undress.

Since assuming my disguise, I had never gone without a jacket in the presence of anyone else. Their padded bulk had been one of the main reasons my masquerade had been successful. I looked now at the coat lying just beyond the reach of my fingertips and glanced sideways at Lord Leyburn. He was squinting up at the sun, a blade of grass between his teeth. Cautiously I stretched my hand forward toward the jacket.

Strong fingers closed like a vise around my

wrist and held my arm rigid. I sat as still as stone and stared at our two bare arms.

I had always been fair but, against the darkness of the earl's hand, my skin looked pearly, translucent almost. The fragile bones and tendons of my arm were in stark contrast to the hardness of the male forearm and hand that gripped it so efficiently. He must have been able to feel the hammering of the pulse in my wrist.

He twisted my arm a little so that I had to turn toward him. I felt his eyes on the open collar of my shirt. I had always been very careful to wear a muffling cravat. Those dark eyes moved from my throat lower down to the chest, and I could feel hot color staining my cheeks.

"All right," he said. "I want the truth. Now."

It was a voice I had never heard from him before. I glanced at him quickly and felt myself recoil from what I saw in his eyes.

"I told you the truth, my lord. The only thing I neglected to mention was my disguise. Everything else was true. I swear it!"

"Who are your grandparents?"

I had guarded that secret for so long, but things were different now. I had never seen him like this.

"Grandpapa is the Earl of Ardsley," I said. "My real name is Valentine Langley."

He let my wrist go and the blood began to flow back into my hand. "Your father?"

"Papa was Captain Francis Langley. He was in the cavalry rear guard that held the French at the Rio Seco during the retreat to Corunna. Papa never made Corunna. He died at the river."

I was afraid to look at him, afraid to see the deadly controlled rage that narrowed his eyes and thinned his mouth. There was an excruciating silence.

"Is it so terrible that I am a girl?" I asked at last in a low voice. My head was beginning to pound. "It isn't my fault that no one would hire me to look after horses if I told the truth. It isn't fair that girls should be more dependent than boys. I am perfectly able to look out for myself."

He said something I had never heard before, not even in the army. Then he took my chin in his hand and held my face up to his. I won't cry, I said to myself fiercely, I will *not* cry.

"How could I have been so stupid?" There was such slashing bitterness in his voice that I shivered despite the warm sunshine. He let me go and stood up.

"All right, this is something I am going to have to deal with. I need to think. And I need time to calm down." He gave me a very grim look. "Are you all right walking back by yourself?"

"Of course I am, my lord. I do it all the time."

The eyes looking at me were very hard and very black. "You go straight to your room when you get home, young lady, and stay there until I tell you otherwise."

I bowed my head. "Yes, my lord." I didn't look up until the sound of hoofbeats told me he had gone.

I walked home in abject misery. My head felt heavy, and it hurt from the sun. My legs became harder and harder to move. It was very hot, but I put my jacket on because I was beginning to shiver.

When I reached home, I had only one desire: to do as his lordship had ordered and get to my room. I undressed and crawled into the big soft bed, where I immediately fell asleep.

I awoke to a cool hand on my cheek. I opened heavy eyelids to see Lord Leyburn's face close above mine. He had been saying my name.

"I—I don't feel very well, my lord," I whispered.

"You have a fever." His voice sounded matter-of-fact and calm. "We'll have the doctor in to give you something." He smoothed the hair back off my hot forehead. "Now, sit up a minute and drink this."

He slipped an arm behind me and raised me up against his shoulder. At the foot of the bed I saw Mr. Fitzallan and Mrs. Emerson, the housekeeper. I drank the lemonade the earl was holding to my lips and looked up into his face.

"I'm sorry," I whispered.

He nodded gravely and lowered me back onto the pillow. I closed my eyes.

I remember very little of the next few days. I was very far away from Carlton Castle, reliving over and over again the terrible moment when word had come to Lisbon that there had been a great battle at Corunna and the English dependents must evacuate.

I hadn't known if my father was alive or dead until I reached London. In my delirium I saw again and again the worried unhappy face of Major Benning saying, "I'm sorry to have to tell you this, Miss Langley, but your father is dead."

"Papa!" I cried out in anguish. "No! Don't leave me!"

And a well-loved voice that was not my father's would answer. "It's all right, Valentine. You're safe. Everything is going to be all right."

Then I was in Newmarket. "I can ride that horse," I said. "Just let me try. I'll show you. I can ride him."

It was very hot. Why was it so hot? I tried to push the heavy blanket off me and someone pushed it back. "Don't do that," I said.

A woman's voice said, "Leave the blankets be, miss. Sit up now, it's time for your medicine."

But I pushed the hands away. "Leave me alone," I said fretfully. "I have to get up. Mama is sick and she needs me."

"Oh, my lord." The woman's voice sounded relieved. "She's been trying to get up."

I was sitting up in bed staring around me in bewilderment. "Where am I?" I asked.

"You're here with me," the familiar voice answered. He put an arm around my shoulder. "Lie down now, sweetheart. You're sick and you need to rest."

I stared up at the dark face so close to mine. "Don't leave me," I whispered.

"No, I won't leave you. Will you take some medicine now?"

"Yes." I opened my mouth for the spoon he was holding.

When next I awoke, it was night. The only light in the room came from the fire, and seated in front of it was the figure of a woman.

"What time is it?" I asked.

She stood up and came over to the bed. "How are you feeling, miss?"

"Tired," I answered. "Who are you?"

"Mrs. Willis, the nurse Lord Leyburn engaged to look after you. You've been sick, but the fever broke earlier in the night. You're going to be all right."

I ran my tongue across my lips. They were dry and cracked. "What time is it?" I repeated.

"Four in the morning, miss. Would you like a drink?"

I was very thirsty. "Yes," I said, and pushed myself up against the pillow. I drank thirstily. "How long have I been sick?"

"Five days, miss. It was the influenza. It's been that bad this year."

"Oh." I tried to smile at her. "I don't remember very much."

"You were delirious, miss."

I had to ask it. "Was—was Lord Leyburn here?"

"Aye. He was the only one we could get you to mind." She took the glass away. "Go back to sleep, miss. There's no need to fret now. You're on the mend."

I closed my eyes and slipped into a deep sleep that for the first time in five days was dreamless.

10

I didn't see Lord Leyburn for the next three days. During that time I was kept in bed and looked after most efficiently by Mrs. Willis. In fact, Mrs. Willis was the only person I saw, aside from the doctor. On the fourth day I was allowed to get up for a short time, and while Mrs. Willis was out of the room, I got dressed in my old clothes and slipped down to the kitchen.

Mrs. Scone and Crosby were sitting at the kitchen table when I walked in and Robert was busy in the corner polishing silver.

"Miss Valentine," Crosby said woodenly, and rose to his feet. "You oughtn't to be here, miss."

Well, I had known it wasn't going to be easy. I looked as pathetic as I could, and with my white, too-thin face and shadowed eyes, I must have looked piteous indeed.

"Oh," I said very sadly. "Am I in disgrace with you, too?"

"That was quite a nasty trick you played on us all, Valentine," Mrs. Scone said sternly. But she had forgotten the miss.

"I know." I drooped as much as I could. "But after my papa was killed, I had nowhere to go, Mrs. Scone. I didn't mean to trick you. I only wanted a job. Please don't hate me."

"Nobody hates you, Miss Valentine." Crosby was beginning to sound quite fatherly. "You were very naughty to deceive us all like that, but certainly no one hates you."

"I'm terribly hungry, Mrs. Scone. I don't see how I'm ever to get better if I'm not allowed to eat anything."

"I sent you up a nice dish of gruel, Valentine."

"Gruel!" I made a face. "I mean real food. I'm *hungry.*"

"Sit you down here, then, and I'll get you something," Mrs. Scone said, and bustled off toward the pantry. Crosby looked at his watch and left the kitchen as well, leaving me alone with Robert. I sat down at the table and looked at him. He was industriously polishing and refused to look back.

"Are you angry with me, Robert?" I asked.

"Certainly not, miss."

"Then why won't you look at me?"

He glanced up from his polishing. "Yes, miss?" he said with implacable politeness.

This was going to be more difficult than Mrs. Scone and Crosby. Robert was palpably unmoved by my pathetic appearance.

"You're just annoyed because it was a girl who beat you at cards," I said.

His lips tightened and his blue eyes glared. "That's not true!"

"Yes, it is. Your pride is hurt, that's all. I'm sorry I had to fool you, but I don't see why you're so upset. What difference does it make, anyway?"

He put down the candlestick he had been polishing for the last five minutes. "What difference? What difference when you let us all think you were a boy when really . . ." He glared even harder. "How could you, Val? How could you?"

This was much better. "Well, Robert, who would have hired a girl to look after a horse?"

"That's not the point."

"Yes it is. It's the whole point, don't you see? After my father was killed, I had to have somewhere to live, some way to earn money."

"You must have relatives. The Quality are never just thrown on the world like that."

"All I have are my grandparents. And they cast my mother off when she married Papa. I'd rather take care of horses than be beholden to them."

"But, Val, don't you see . . ." Robert was beginning when Mrs. Scone came back with a plate of cheese and freshly cut bread.

I smiled. "This looks delicious, Mrs. Scone."

I really was starving and was halfway through the cheese when Mrs. Willis appeared to drag me off.

"Let the lass finish her meal," Mrs. Scone told the nurse firmly. Mrs. Willis took exception to her tone and her interference, and while the two women battled it out, I finished the bread and cheese. As Mrs. Willis finally led me off, I looked back over my shoulder at Robert and winked. He grinned, caught Mrs. Scone's eye on him, and went back to polishing the silver.

The following day Mrs. Emerson, the housekeeper, came into my bedroom with a stack of boxes.

"His lordship sent me into Richmond to buy some proper clothes for you, Miss Valentine. I had to guess your size, but these should be adequate for a while. It won't do for you to be wearing those boy's clothes any longer." And she gave me a severely disapproving look.

"Yes, ma'am," I said meekly. I was sitting up in bed and reading a book.

"Get up and we'll try these on."

I hopped out of bed with alacrity and looked

with interest through Mrs. Emerson's boxes. There were stockings and underwear and shoes and gloves and three dresses. The dresses were all rather big as were the shoes.

"There's nothing to you, lass," Mrs. Emerson said as she pulled a blue muslin this way and that.

"I lost weight when I was sick, I think."

"Well, I'll have Rose take a stitch or two in these for you. His lordship is going to send you into York to get a proper wardrobe, so these will only have to do temporarily."

"They are very pretty dresses, Mrs. Emerson," I assured her. I looked at myself in the mirror. The dresses might be pretty, but one could hardly say the same thing of the wearer. With my ragged head and too-thin face, I looked like an underfed urchin. "I don't know what I can do about my hair," I said dismally.

Mrs. Emerson surveyed me critically. "Sit down here, Miss Valentine, and I'll trim it for you."

I sat down on the chair and Mrs. Emerson began to comb my hair, trying it first one way and then another.

"It doesn't curl," I informed her.

"It's very fine for all it's so thick," she returned, picked up the scissors, and began to snip away.

Ten minutes later she said, "There, that looks

better," and stepped back to look at me. I turned to the mirror.

She had trimmed my bangs and cut the rest of my hair so it fell back away from my face. It was quite short on the sides but grew longer on the back of my neck.

"Well," I said doubtfully, "it looks much neater. Thank you."

"It's very pretty hair," the housekeeper said unexpectedly. "A lovely color, really, all brown and coppery and gold, like the autumn leaves."

It was very nice of her to try to cheer me up and I smiled gratefully. She picked up her scissors and went to the door.

"You're much too pale, my dear. I suggest you take that book of yours and go sit in the garden for a little. You need to put the color back into those cheeks."

"I will, Mrs. Emerson. And thank you."

It felt wonderful to be outdoors again, and I held my face up to the warmth of the sun and closed my eyes.

"You look like a little flower soaking up the sun like that," said a deep voice close to me. It was not the voice I was longing to hear, but I opened my eyes and smiled.

Mr. Fitzallan sat down next to me on the stone bench and asked, "How are you, Valentine?"

"Much better, thank you." I looked up at his profile. "Was it so very terrible a thing to have done?" I ventured.

He didn't answer my question. "Diccon tells me Lord Ardsley is your grandfather."

"Yes." There was a long silence and then I asked, "Has—has his lordship told them I am here?"

"Not yet." Mr. Fitzallan looked down at me impassively. "I will never understand why you did not do as your father wished and go to them, Valentine."

I bit my lip. "Lord Leyburn understood. He said he would have done the same."

"That was before he knew the truth."

"But what difference can it make?" I cried. "*I am still the same. Why can't we just go on as we were?*"

He smiled a little ruefully. "What a child you are, Valentine." Then he too, as Lord Leyburn had done, took my chin in his hand and tilted my face up. "Once one knows, it's hard to see how you could have fooled us," he murmured. His touch was very gentle, and as he released my chin, he touched my cheek. "You have no idea, do you, of the problem your disguise has visited on poor Diccon?"

"What problem?"

He shrugged and stood up. "I'll let him explain it to you. Stay out here a little longer. You need some color in your face. You're too pale." He smiled. "You were a very sick girl, you know."

I watched him walk back to the house. He was right. I had no idea of what a problem my disguise might cause, nor did I particularly care. The only thing I did care about was the information that Lord Leyburn had not written as yet to my grandparents. And he was going to buy me some clothes. Perhaps—perhaps that meant I would be allowed to stay. . . .

I did not see Lord Leyburn for two more days. He was not at home, Mrs. Emerson informed me, but she did not know where he had gone.

When I finally received a message that his lordship wished to see me in the library, my heart lurched and my palms grew damp. I had to be allowed to stay, I thought fiercely, and I was not thinking of my dislike of my grandparents. I was thinking that my heart would break if I were never to see Lord Leyburn again.

He was standing at the far side of the room when I arrived in the open doorway of the library. His back was to me and my eyes went over him hungrily, over the wide shoulders that narrowed into such slim hips and long strong legs. I took a deep breath. The last time he had spoken he had been so angry.

"You wished to see me, my lord?"

He turned. Nobody in the world looked like

Richard Fitzallan. The sunshine slanting in the window fell full on his hair. It was absolutely black. There was not a trace of brown or of red in it. He did not look angry, but his eyes were veiled by his lashes and I had no way of telling what he was thinking.

"Yes," he said. "Come in, Valentine."

I advanced slowly into the room, painfully aware of my baggy dress and my cropped hair. I had never felt self-conscious with him before.

"You look like a startled fawn," he said. "Don't worry, sweetheart, I'm not going to shout at you." He sounded amused and my eyes flew to meet his. He *was* amused.

"Oh, my lord," I said in a rush. "I'm so sorry I tricked you, but truly I didn't see any other way. No one would hire a girl."

"Not to look after their horses at any rate," he said dryly.

I began to feel better. "No. And I really was not in the market for the only job I could have gotten otherwise."

"How old are you?"

"Eighteen, my lord."

"Christ, you don't look it." He moved to his favorite seat and said to me, "Sit down."

I was feeling much better. He wasn't angry and he hadn't contacted my grandfather. Or had he?

"You do still understand why I didn't want to

live with my grandparents, don't you?" I asked cautiously.

"Oh, I understand that, all right. I've met your grandfather, you know."

"Is he awful?"

"He's perfectly godly, righteous, and sober."

"He's awful," I said. "I knew it."

"At any rate, he's not your kind, Valentine."

"No," I said complacently. "I'm like my father."

"I'm very much afraid," Lord Leyburn said slowly, "that you are going to have to remain here."

"Oh, *thank* you, my lord!" I leapt to my feet, and before I quite knew what I was doing, I was kneeling next to his chair. "I'll be good, I promise you I will be. I'll do everything you ask. Truly." His hand was lying on the arm of his chair and impulsively I picked it up and kissed the hard masculine fingers.

He looked at me very gravely. "You don't quite understand the situation, Valentine. You are going to have to marry me."

I wasn't sure I had heard him correctly. "What —what did you say, my lord?"

He turned so that I was kneeling upright in front of him. He took both my hands in his and said, "You have been living in my house for months, unchaperoned. There is no way your reputation can survive that, sweetheart. I'm afraid you have no alternative but to marry me."

"But—but no one knew I was a girl."

He shrugged. "Who will believe that? Looking at you now, I wouldn't believe it myself."

I knelt there, my hands in his. So this was the problem Mr. Fitzallan had alluded to. "Marry you?" I said dazedly.

"Yes. You have no choice in the matter, Valentine. Ned offered, but you and Ned would not do at all." He smiled. "Poor Ned, it's enough that he has to put up with me. He doesn't need a wife who'll do his thinking for him as well."

"But you're going to marry Lady Barbara Bevil," I said.

"Not anymore, I'm not." He leaned forward and kissed me, very gently, on the lips. "As I said before, Valentine, you have no choice, and neither do I. Perhaps if you were younger, but eighteen . . . No, there is no way out of it but marriage."

He had kissed me as if I were a child. My kiss on his hands had been far more passionate. He didn't want to marry me; he only thought he had to. I pulled my hands away and stood up.

"No," I said. "It's—it's ridiculous. I never meant anything like this to happen. I feel as if I've—I've trapped you. I won't do it. It's ridiculous."

"Unfortunately, it is not ridiculous. It's the

way of the world." He stood up as well. "It won't be so bad, sweetheart," he said confidently.

Won't be so bad! If only he knew . . .

"My lord," I began.

"You may as well call me Diccon," he said easily. He patted my cheek. "No more discussion, now. The matter is settled. I've been to see the archbishop about getting a special license. I think we'd be wise to notify your grandparents after the wedding. I'll think up some tale to satisfy their puritan consciences."

"But—"

"Just think," he said. "You'll be the first countess whose servants are all on a first-name basis with her." He laughed and went to the door. "You still look very peaked," he said from the doorway. "I'll take you out for a drive this afternoon. At three. Be ready, please." He was gone.

11

I went upstairs to my room, sat down on the window seat and stared out at the beautiful day. I had never felt so absolutely alone in my life, not even when my father died.

I could have it, the dearest wish of my heart. I could stay here at Carlton Castle for the rest of my life. I could be the wife of the man I loved, the only man I would ever love. I should be jumping with joy.

And yet . . . I loved him but he did not love me. Oh, he cared for me. I didn't doubt that. I was his little companion: young Valentine, who so obviously admired and idolized him. He was accustomed to hero worship, however, and did not take it too seriously. He thought I was amusing and he enjoyed my way of looking at life. He thought I was a child. And I knew I was not.

I was unsophisticated, I didn't doubt that. It had never crossed my mind that my disguise could place Lord Leyburn—I was afraid to think of him as Diccon, even to myself—in such a difficult position. I was unsophisticated and thoughtless, but I was not a child—not where he was concerned, at any rate. I knew what I wanted from him. I felt it in my blood every time he looked at me.

It would be terrible for him to have to marry a girl he didn't want and then to find himself the object of a passionate and possessive love. I am not a lukewarm person. I wanted it all or I wanted nothing. I could bear to live with him as a sort of young sister; I could not live with him as his wife.

I could not marry him.

I could not tell him why I couldn't marry him.

I would have to run away again.

The more I thought about it, however, the more difficult that course of action appeared. I could not simply steal a horse and gallop off to my grandparents. Lord Leyburn would be after me as soon as I was missed. He knew the roads much better than I. Without a doubt he would catch me.

I would have to go to my grandparents. I would have to be able to assure Lord Leyburn that I was safe and protected and that his very generous offer was entirely unnecessary. They were the only circumstances under which he would be able to consider himself released from his responsibility to me.

The problem was: how was I to get to my grandparents in Lincolnshire? I was still undecided about that when three o'clock came around.

I didn't have anything to change into that was more appropriate than what I had on, so I went downstairs to meet his lordship dressed as I was. He was not yet in the hall, but the phaeton was at the door. Georgie was holding the horses and I went out to greet him.

"Hello, Georgie," I said glumly.

He had straightened as soon as he saw me. "Good afternoon, miss."

Quite suddenly I was furious. "Don't you start that, too," I snapped. "I am still the same person I was. *I* haven't changed, it's everyone else who has changed toward me. I have never met more snobs in my life than among the people who work here. You make the army look democratic." I glared at him.

"But, miss," he began.

"Don't you dare 'miss' me!" I shouted.

Quite suddenly he began to grin. "You're right, Val. You're still the same. But that dress is much too big for you."

I looked down at my person. "I know. I look awful. I wish to God I could have my breeches back."

"Hutchins had a fit when he found out about you," Georgie offered.

"Did he?" I leaned against the phaeton. "What did he say?"

We were both laughing when Lord Leyburn came down the front steps. Once again Georgie snapped to attention and his lordship gave him a preoccupied nod.

"Ready, Valentine?" he asked me.

"I have been ready since three o'clock. As you requested, my lord."

"I'm sorry to be late," he said, and his mouth curled down a little at the corners. He was amused.

"That is quite all right," I replied grandly. "Georgie and I have been having a very interesting conversation."

His eyes narrowed. He thought I was funny. I stuck my chin in the air and looked over his shoulder.

"May I help you into the phaeton, Valentine?" He sounded very courteous. Too courteous.

"Thank you." I extended my hand.

He didn't take it. Instead, he put his hands on my waist and lifted me into the seat. I looked down at him, surprised to be where I was, and he said gravely, "You're welcome." Behind him I

saw Georgie grinning. I gave them both a wither-
ing look and settled my skirts. I could still feel
the warmth of his hands on my waist.

We had been driving for five minutes before he
spoke. "You're too thin, you know. You weigh
scarcely anything. Aren't you eating?"

"I lost weight when I was sick. I'll gain it back
soon enough."

I took my hat off and let the breeze ruffle my
hair. I didn't look at him. It hurt too much.

"We shouldn't delay this wedding for too long,
Valentine," he said after a few minutes. "I've got
the license."

I stared at my blue skirts and suddenly I had an
idea. Bless Georgie, I thought.

"I refuse to get married in these clothes," I said
firmly.

"What?"

"You heard what I said. Everyone has been
telling me how dreadful they make me look.
Even you, just now, you said I look skinny. It's
not that I'm so skinny, it's that these dresses are
too big."

"Valentine, no one cares if your dress is too
big," he began patiently.

"I care. Mrs. Emerson said you were going to
send me into York to have some clothes fitted
properly."

He stopped the phaeton and turned to look at

me. "After the wedding, sweetheart, you can have all the clothes you want. I'll take you to York myself. But first we must be married."

"No."

There was a flicker of impatience across his face, and I clenched my hands in my lap. "You will do as I say." His voice was unnervingly quiet.

Mr. Fitzallan was right, I thought. He got his own way too damn often. "No, I will not." I kept my own voice equally quiet. "Mrs. Emerson and I will go into York to buy me some new clothes and *then* we will be married." His mouth thinned a little and suddenly I lost my temper. "Don't you dare try to bully me!" My voice was no longer quiet. "I will not be married in this hideous dress. And it's sheer bloody unfeeling arrogance on your part to try to make me do it."

I sat rigid, braced for a blast of anger, and was astonished when his face relaxed and he began to smile. "All right, Valentine. Have it your way." He raised a very black eyebrow and gave me a look of mock disapproval. "There was no need to swear," he said. "Wherever did you learn such language?"

"From you," I replied promptly.

He laughed softly, as if to himself, and then started up the horses again. I watched him out of the corner of my eye, drinking in the splendid, clear profile, the long straight nose, the firm mouth and arched brow. I felt swept with anguish.

"What were you and Georgie talking about?" he asked.

"Hutchins." I told him what Georgie had told me about the head groom's reaction to my unmasking, and he found it as funny as I had.

"Hutchins has a very low opinion of females," he said when he had finished laughing.

"Do you know, I really think that girls could do most of the things boys do if they were given the chance."

A small smile lingered on his mouth. "I don't know about that, Valentine."

"The problem is," I said forcefully, "men have all the fun and they don't want to share it."

He looked at me curiously. "Did you have fun, being a boy?"

"Yes, I did. I learned how to throw dice and how to play cards and—"

He was shouting with laughter. "All the good things in life."

"Well, they are fun. Better than sewing samplers and learning embroidery, which is what girls have to do."

"I can't picture you sewing a sampler."

"Actually, I never did," I confessed. "It wasn't my style."

"No, I can see that."

"I'm afraid I'm a very undisciplined person." I sighed.

"I wouldn't say that at all." He sounded very serious now. "I would say you were courageous and generous and independent. Too independent, perhaps. You're a bit too fond of your own way."

My jaw dropped. *"I'm* fond of my own way." I stared at his profile in astonished indignation.

He shook his head sadly. "Willful. That's what you are."

"Do you know what you are?" I asked sweetly.

"No." He looked at me. "Tell me," he invited.

We had never spoken on such a personal level before. There was a new note to this conversation and I knew it was dangerous. He thought my feelings for him were simple hero worship. I did not want to betray anything further.

"I wouldn't dream of venturing into such complicated territory," I said flatly. "Are you going to try to race Saladin or just use him at stud?"

There was a moment of quiet. "Stud, I think," he said then, and our conversation fell into a more ordinary path. I kept it there, with some difficulty, throughout the remainder of our drive.

12

I joined Lord Leyburn and his cousin for dinner that evening. It was my first experience sitting down in the huge dining room, and I felt very strange as Lord Leyburn took his seat at the head of the table across from me. The table had all its leaves removed, but there was still quite a large expanse of mahogany between us.

I looked up to find both men watching me. "Such lovely weather we've been having lately," I said.

Mr. Fitzallan looked startled.

"A little too dry, perhaps," his lordship murmured.

"Indeed?" Robert put a bowl of soup in front

of me. "I didn't think the English weather could ever be too dry."

"Oh, there have been droughts upon occasion," Lord Leyburn returned.

I looked up from my soup and caught his eye. Quite suddenly my sense of strangeness disappeared. "If I asked you the dates, would you give them to me?"

"Of course."

I grinned. "Then I won't ask."

"Thank heavens." It was Mr. Fitzallan and we both laughed.

"Eat your soup, Valentine," his lordship said exactly as if I had been ten years old.

I gave him a look but obediently picked up my spoon. It was oxtail soup, one of my favorites.

"You can leave for York tomorrow," his lordship said, and at his words my appetite fled.

"York?" said Mr. Fitzallan.

"Valentine has informed me that she refuses to be married in a gown that makes her look like a famine victim."

Robert was standing directly behind Lord Leyburn, and I could see quite clearly the look of shock on his face. It was evidently the first time he had heard of my proposed marriage. It was a look that stayed with me, and when the main course had been served and the servants left the room, I brought the subject up.

"Robert looked as if he were going to have apoplexy when you mentioned our marriage, my lord. How can I possibly run the house when I've played cards with half the footmen?"

"Not to mention dicing with the grooms," he murmured.

"Valentine," said Mr. Fitzallan reproachfully, "you didn't."

"She did." His lordship drank some wine and looked at me. "Who usually won?" he asked.

"I did."

He grinned. "I knew it." He turned to Mr. Fitzallan. "Did you enjoy the soup, Ned?"

Mr. Fitzallan looked surprised by the change of topic. "Well, it was not my favorite," he said doubtfully.

"It's my favorite," I put in stoutly. "And I think Mrs. Scone makes it excellently."

"Is stuffed capon another favorite of yours?" his lordship asked.

"Yes, it is."

His dark eyes were filled with the light of the candles. "You're running the house already," he told me. "All you need to do is flash that amazing smile of yours and they'll run like slaves to do whatever you want."

I stared at him in utter astonishment.

"Those big blue eyes don't hurt either," commented Mr. Fitzallan.

I turned said eyes on his face. He was smiling.

"You're teasing me," I said reproachfully.

"Only a little," said his lordship. "You were never regarded as one of them by the servants and you know it."

I looked at him across the candles. "I suppose so," I whispered. For a long moment we looked at each other and then my eyes fell. I was grateful when Mr. Fitzallan changed the topic.

I did not sleep well that night, and by the time Lord Leyburn handed me into the coach in the morning I was so exhausted and so concerned with keeping my face expressionless that I scarcely took in the fact that I was saying goodbye to him forever. I could not even let down my guard after the coach had driven away from the door because Mrs. Emerson was there, chatting comfortably about all the nice things we were going to buy.

I had never been to York before, and under any other circumstances I would have been delighted with the walled city that still retained a distinct air of the Middle Ages.

"York was a capital city while London was still a village," Lord Leyburn had said to me, but now, instead of drinking in the sight of the magnificent minster and the ancient walls and gates, all I was concerned with was how to find the stagecoach office and how I was going to slip away from Mrs. Emerson.

Lord Leyburn had given me a handsome sum of money to spend over and above whatever bills I ran up at the dressmaker, so I was not short of blunt. Mrs. Emerson and I settled quite comfortably into the Fitzallan town residence with plans to begin our shopping in the morning.

In the morning I told Mrs. Emerson that I was not feeling well. She wanted to summon a doctor, but I said it was only a headache and begged her to leave me alone to sleep it away.

"I'm sure I shall feel better this afternoon," I assured her. "Please, do go out yourself. I shall be so upset if I think I've kept you from enjoying your visit."

In the end she did go out. I stuffed my few dresses in a bag and sat down to compose a note to Lord Leyburn. When I had finished it, I read it over before propping it on the mantel with a note to Mrs. Emerson to deliver it to his lordship personally.

Dear Lord Leyburn:

I am afraid I have run away again and this time to the people I should have gone to in the first place. I have gone to my grandparents. I have no intention of telling them where I have been for the last few months so no one need know of our association.

My dearest lord, you know you don't want to marry me. Nor do I want to serve you such a trick after all your kindness to me. We were friends, I think, and I should like to go on thinking of you in that light.

Please do not come after me. If you do, you will ruin everything. If I find things do not fall out as I expect, I promise most faithfully to let you know. I'm quite certain my grandparents will take me in, however. What choice will they have when I arrive bag and baggage on their doorstep?

Valentine

P.S. I'm afraid you won't see your money again. I need it for the coach.

That should do it, I thought. Mrs. Emerson wouldn't open a letter addressed to Lord Leyburn, and by the time she got back to Carlton to deliver it, I would be at Ardsley. I took one last look around and then sneaked out of my room and down the stairs. There was no one in the front hall, so I was able to make at least a partially dignified exit from the Earl of Leyburn's town house.

I had decided to go to an inn in the hopes of being able to get a seat on either a stagecoach or the mail. As it happened, luck was with me, for the mail came thundering into the White Boar only fifteen minutes after my arrival, and it was going through Lincoln on its way to London. I got the last seat.

It wasn't until I was bouncing along in the

safety of the crowded coach that I put my mind to what I was going to tell my grandparents.

In Lincoln I hired a coach to take me to Stainfield, where I knew my grandparents resided. Their house proved to be very different from the great and ancient castle inhabited by the Earl of Leyburn. Ardsley was a Palladian mansion, its style classical and dignified. The park, with its ornamental lake and carefully laid out trees and shrubbery, provided a serene and gracious setting for the smooth, pale stone house. I got out of the coach and looked with some misgivings at the austere and symmetrical pillars of the front entry. I was terribly conscious of my cropped head and my baggy dress. I squared my shoulders.

"Are you sure this is where you want to go, miss?" the driver asked me.

"Yes," I said dismally.

"You sure you don't want me to wait for you?"

"Yes." I looked at him ruefully. "They'll have to take me in, you see. I'm a relation."

"Hmph. That don't mean nothin', miss," he informed me. "They know you're coming?"

"No."

"I'll wait awhile," he said, and settled back on his seat and crossed his arms.

I had to smile. "That's very kind of you," I said, and began to walk up the front stairs. I really didn't have too many doubts that I would be turned away. Papa had told me to come and I was quite certain Papa had made previous arrangements. I rapped the knocker.

A very proper-looking butler answered.

"Good afternoon," I said. "I have come to see Lord and Lady Ardsley. I am Valentine Langley, their granddaughter."

The starchy look on the butler's face altered. He held the door open.

"Come in, miss. I will inform my lady that you have arrived." I turned and waved to my faithful coachman before I followed the butler into the house.

13

I was ushered into a very elegant, silk-covered room, and the butler disappeared. I sat down on a fragile-looking chair, very different from the massive carved furniture that was so in evidence at Carlton Castle, and stared into space.

The door opened and an elegantly dressed and coiffed silver-haired lady came in. I stood up.

"Valentine?" she said, and looked at me as if I were an extremely unsatisfactory footman.

"Yes." I looked her over as well. "You are Lady Ardsley?"

"I am your grandmother." She came across the room to stand in front of me. Up close she looked much older. She was several inches shorter than

I. "Where have you been?" she demanded. "We received notice of your father's death months ago."

She was every bit as bad as I thought she would be. I smiled. "Please don't exhaust yourself with condolences, Grandmother."

She gave me an icy stare. "Don't be impertinent. I never liked your father. You must know that. He ruined my daughter's life. Now, *where have you been these last months?* Your father's colonel was very upset by your disappearance. As were your grandfather and I."

"My father did not ruin Mama's life," I said flatly. "I have been staying with my old nurse and trying to get a job as governess."

"*What?*"

Oh, lord, I thought. If she's upset by the thought of my being a governess, I can imagine what she'd say if she knew the truth.

"That's right. But no one would hire me. I'm too young."

"Sit down, Valentine." We both seated ourselves and regarded each other warily. "Did your father not tell you that in the event of his death you were to come to Ardsley?"

"You never even wrote to my mother," I said woodenly. "Not once. She told me."

The old face in front of me became exceedingly stern. "I told Elizabeth how it would be if she went against our wishes and married that boy. She chose her bed. It seems she came to regret her choice."

"She did not," I said fiercely.

We stared at each other and then my grandmother said, "Am I to understand, then, that having failed to find employment on your own, you have humbled your pride and come to us?"

The old harridan. She thought she had the upper hand, and was she loving it.

"Was my father mistaken?" I asked. "Are you unwilling to have me?"

"I did not say that."

We were back to staring at each other. If she thought I was going to crawl, she was much mistaken.

"What would you do if I said we did not want you here?" she asked at last.

"Get another kind of job," I replied promptly.

She looked scornful. "What kind of job is open to a girl like you, Valentine?"

I gave her my nicest, my most charming smile. "I could always sell my body," I said.

I thought she was going to choke. When she had got her breath back, she glared at me. "You ill-bred impudent hussy. Don't you dare to speak to me like that."

"I don't like blackmail," I said. "If you wish me to stay, I will endeavor to do my best to be a satisfactory granddaughter to you. I don't promise miracles, mind. I'm only human. But I will try. On the other hand, I will not tolerate unkind remarks about either of my parents, nor will I tolerate being made to feel like a poor relation here on suffrance. If that is to be the situation, I'd prefer to work for my keep."

I folded my hands in my lap and looked at her calmly. "Well, Grandmama, which is it to be? Am I to stay or to go?"

She didn't deign to answer but rose majestically from her chair. "Come along and I'll show you your room. Your grandfather went into Lincoln this morning, so you will not be able to meet him until dinner."

I stood up as well. "Thank you, Grandmama. I should be glad to freshen up."

She looked me over critically. "Whatever have you done to your hair, child? It looks dreadful."

"I know. I was sick and they cut it."

"Sick?" she repeated. "Recently? Is that why you are so thin?"

I sighed. This refrain was becoming rather tedious. "Yes, Grandmama," I said.

"We'll have to feed you up," my grandmother said. "I'll have some nice soup taken up to you right away."

I trailed out of the room after her, reflecting in some astonishment that the whole world seemed to be united in a mission to fatten up Valentine.

* * *

My grandfather was also silver-haired and dignified. He welcomed me temperately but kindly and told me I was too thin.

My grandmother had a dressmaker in and I was fitted for a new wardrobe. My grandmother's hairdresser also looked at my hair and, after shaking her head in horror, produced a style that I rather liked. I thought it made me look sophisticated.

Four days after my arrival I was walking back from a visit to the stable when I heard a voice call from the orchard next to the path.

"Val! Over here, Val!"

I looked and saw a familiar face peering out at me.

"Georgie!" I looked hurriedly around, but no one was near, so I slipped into the trees to join him. "What are you doing here?" I asked in wonder.

"His lordship sent me to find out if you were really here."

"Oh. How—how is he?"

"God." Georgie shivered. "There's been no talking to him, Val. Everyone at Carlton is walking on eggshells."

"Oh, dear. Well, you can tell him I'm just fine, Georgie. My grandparents have been very nice to me. I told them I had been staying with my old nurse, so they know nothing about Carlton or about my disguise."

"Is your grandfather really an earl?" Georgie asked.

"I'm afraid so."

"But *why* . . ." He broke off and then looked at his boots. "Never mind," he mumbled.

"I know," I said. "I should have come here right after my father died. It doesn't make sense to anyone but me why I didn't."

"Well, if I had a grandfather who lived in a house like this, I sure wouldn't run off to be a groom."

"I know," I repeated. "I'm peculiar, I suppose."

"You're not peculiar," said Georgie. "You're just Val, and not like anyone else."

"True," I said glumly. "That's always been my problem."

Georgie grinned. "Well, then, I'll tell his lordship he's not to worry about you."

"That's right. I'm perfectly fine. I'm even getting a new wardrobe."

"You need one," said Georgie.

I made a face at him. "How is everyone else?" I asked, and he gave me all the news of the stable.

"Well, I'd better be going," he said at last, and I had to struggle to keep tears from my eyes. It had been so good to see him.

"Yes, I suppose so." I bit my lip. "I miss you all."

"We miss you too, Val." He sounded suddenly gruff. "It just hasn't been the same at Carlton since you left."

I managed a smile and held out my hand. It was clasped briefly in his hard and calloused one, and then he turned and walked very swiftly through the trees and out of my sight. He had a horse tied near the main road, he had told me. He was heading straight back to Carlton. I wished with all my heart that I was going with him.

PART II

Spring, 1810

Your master quits you; and for your service done him,
So much against the mettle of your sex,
So far beneath your soft and tender breeding
And since you called me master, for so long,
Here is my hand: you shall from this time be
Your master's mistress.

Twelfth Night
V, i, 341-347

14

I had told my grandmother that I would do my best to be a satisfactory granddaughter, and for the following year I conscientiously tried to fulfill my promise. Without wishing to sound smug, I think I was fairly successful.

My grandparents were lonely. It didn't take me long to perceive that they regretted the break with my mother. It was pride that had kept them estranged. If my mother had made the first move toward them, they would have relented. But Mama had had her pride too, I suppose. Really, it was all so stupid. I hoped I should never make myself so unhappy for so little reason.

I recognized my grandparents' loneliness so quickly because it was a state I was familiar with myself. I tried not to think of him. I was not successful. In the midst of all the elegance and beauty of Ardsley, I was possessed by a cold and flinty loneliness that nothing could alleviate. Music was the only thing that helped. My grandparents had a wonderful piano and for hours every day I escaped into the only world I could find comfort in.

In the spring my grandparents took me to London for the Season. I was not reluctant to go. It was the only chance I could see of getting news of Diccon. (In my mind, now, that was how I thought of him. The distance between us made the familiarity seem comforting rather than dangerous.)

The Season was the time of year when all the important members of society descended upon London en masse. Town houses, which bore the names of the families who lived in them, were opened and staffed. Splendid carriages and sporty equippages filled the streets. Gentlemen sat in the windows of their clubs and watched the world go by. The business of government went on in the Houses of Parliament, and every night there were receptions and balls that didn't end until four in the morning.

My grandparents opened up Ardsley House in Grosvenor Square for the first time in years and my grandmother procured for me a voucher for Almack's. Almack's I was solemnly informed, was London's most exclusive social club and parade ground for all the young girls who came to London to find a husband.

"Is that why we're going to London, Grand-mama?" I asked. "So I can find a husband?"

"You will have to marry, Valentine. All girls marry."

This was indisputably true, if somewhat depressing.

"You are certain to find some nice young man," my grandmother went serenely on. "A nice, *suitable* young man," she amended. It was one of the very few references she had ever made to my father. She too was keeping to her part of the bargain.

I was to meet society at a ball given by my grandmother's old friend the Countess of Witton.

"Letty has kept up her ties with the world far more than I," my grandmother informed me. "She always gives one of the opening balls of the Season and she has very kindly agreed to launch you. It will be a wonderful opportunity, Valentine."

I had a beautiful new gown for the Great Occasion: white gauze over a hyacinth blue underskirt. It had a scooped neck and small sleeves, and fell gracefully from a high-cut waist-line. I was still very slim—I had decided gloomily that I was never going to be voluptuous—but I no longer looked skinny. My hair had grown as well, and Grandmama's own dresser had arranged it very nicely off my neck with a spray of blue flowers pinned in the knot she had fastened. I wore pearls and small pearl earrings, and thought I looked rather nice.

Grandmama looked pleased with me and Grandpapa patted my cheek and said I would be the prettiest girl in London. The poor old dears were so happy to have a party to look forward to.

Lady Witton, Grandmama's bosom bow, was absolutely glittering with diamonds when we arrived in Berkeley Square. There was a small dinner party first. I was seated between two elderly gentlemen, one of whom I discovered was at the Horse Guards. We discussed the Peninsula campaign quite happily during most of the courses.

As soon as the rest of the guests began to arrive, Lady Witton stationed herself at the top of her long, curving staircase to receive them. I stood next to her, and beyond me were Grandmama and Grandpapa.

There must have been three hundred people in attendance. I stood there, smiling and shaking hands, and listened in wonder to the stentorian tones of the majordomo as he boomed out the names of the approaching guests. There was a veritable orgy of titles: His Grace of This, the Right Honorable That, Lord and Lady This and

That, His Excellency the Ambassador of Who Knows Where. They went by me in a haze of black and white and flashing jewels and gowns, and no one registered on my consciousness until the majordomo proclaimed, "The Right Honorable Martin Wakefield," and I felt my grandmother stiffen beside me. I looked at her quickly. Wakefield was my grandparents' family name.

"I don't believe you've ever met your cousin," Lady Witton was saying to the young man before her. Then she turned to me. "Valentine, allow me to present a cousin of yours, Martin Wakefield."

I held out my hand. "How do you do. I didn't know I had a cousin."

Martin Wakefield smiled. He was noticeably handsome, with a fresh-colored face and smooth blond hair. He took my hand in his and held it.

"I didn't know I had a cousin like you," he returned. There was unabashed admiration in his gray eyes and I smiled back.

"How have you been, Martin?" said my grandmother, and he dropped my hand and turned to speak to her. She looked a little frostier than usual, I thought, but she was very civil to him.

Finally there was a break in the stream of guests and Lady Witton turned to my grandmother. "You can take this child into the ballroom now, Mary."

My grandmother nodded. "Come along, Valentine. You are to open the dancing."

"I am?"

"Yes. Would you like to lead off with the Duke of Wellfleet?"

"Oh, no. I want to dance with Grandpapa first. Please."

The poor love looked absolutely delighted and with gallant courtesy offered me his arm. We went onto the floor and the orchestra started up. The ball was officially open.

It was quite a nice dance, and rather to my own surprise, I found myself enjoying it. I danced twice with my newfound cousin and I enjoyed talking to him as well.

"Why is it I've never heard of you?" I asked him as we went into supper together.

"Your grandfather does not approve of me." He gave me a strange slanting look and added, "I don't suppose you know, then, that I'm his heir?"

"Are you?" I looked at him thoughtfully. "Is that why Grandpapa doesn't approve of you?"

He grinned. He had a very engaging smile. "No. It's my politics that infuriate him so."

"And what are your politics?"

"Your grandfather would call me a radical."

This was intriguing. "What do you propose that is so radical?"

"Change," he said wryly.

"Oh, dear. I suppose you are a Whig?"

"Well, at any rate, I sit in the Commons and always vote against the Tories."

"I see your problem," I sympathized.

"Uncle George cannot bear the thought that someday I will be Lord Ardsley. The Wakefields have always been a strictly reactionary, intensely class-conscious family. He regards me as a black sheep."

"The poor dear," I murmured. "He has a fatal talent for making himself unhappy."

He looked at me curiously. "What do you mean?"

"He fell out with my mother because he thought she had married beneath her," I explained. "And he has apparently alienated you as well. And the person who has suffered the most from these estrangements is himself. And Grandmama too, of course. It is really too bad."

We sat down at a little table. "Well, now they have you," he said.

"Yes." I tried the lobster patties. They were delicious. "The poor old dears are pathetically glad to have a young person about the place."

"Well, they were the ones who banished your mother," he said a little grimly. "God, these old families and their obsession with class."

"Not all old families are like that," I said, and thought of one particular family and one particular person.

"Oh, oh. Here they come." My cousin rose to his feet as my grandparents approached. They both looked extremely dignified and not at all pathetic.

"I am glad to see you and Valentine are getting acquainted, Martin," my grandmother said graciously.

Martin looked so surprised that I had to stifle a giggle. "May I get you a plate of food, Aunt Mary?" he asked.

"Thank you, dear boy."

The dear boy exchanged a mystified look with me and took himself off. When he returned, he sat down again and the four of us made a very pleasant family party.

"This is certainly a change of tune," Martin muttered to me as he escorted me back into the ballroom.

"Haven't you tumbled to it yet?" I asked.

He stared at me blankly. "Tumbled to what?"

"The heir and the granddaughter," I said *sotto voce*. "The old dears are matchmaking."

His brows flew up. "So that's it, by Jove."

"Of course it is." I smiled at him cheerfully. "Don't worry, Martin. I'm not out to catch you."

He assumed an exaggerated expression of hurt.

"Now you've injured my feelings," he complained. "I'm not so bad a fellow."

I laughed. "We'll see," I said teasingly. "We'll see."

15

The day after Lady Witton's ball four bouquets of flowers were delivered to Ardsley House for me; Grandmama was delighted. The four gentlemen who sent the flowers all came to call, and I sat sedately in the drawing room and made conversation. Late in the afternoon Martin took me for a drive in the park and that evening there was another ball. Life in London appeared to be a continual round of social activity.

I was dancing with Martin at Almack's one evening two weeks after my presentation when there was a little flutter of excitement around the dance floor. I followed most people's eyes and looked toward the door. Standing there was the most beautiful girl I had ever seen. Her hair was like spun gold and the blue of her eyes was visible all the way across the room. I looked up at Martin.

"Who is that?"

He smiled a little crookedly. "That is Lady Barbara Bevil, better known as The Beauty."

"Isn't—isn't she the Duke of Cartington's daughter?"

"She is."

We danced in silence and my mind was in a whirl from which only one thought emerged clearly: she wasn't married, she was still Lady Barbara Bevil and not the Countess of Leyburn.

"Leyburn," said Martin, and I started violently to hear my own thoughts echoed.

"What did you say?"

"I said Leyburn didn't come up to scratch over the winter, apparently. Perhaps this Season her father will listen to another offer."

"Leyburn?" I asked tentatively.

"The Earl of Leyburn. Good God, Valentine, surely you know that name. The Fitzallans make the Wakefields look modern."

"Of course I know the name."

"Well, the old duke has been trying to arrange a match between Lady Barbara and the earl. They're still frightfully dynastic up there in the north."

"Does he ever come to London?" I asked a little breathlessly. "Lord Leyburn, I mean."

"Very rarely. I know I've never seen him. And a good thing it is, too, that he keeps away. Talk about a throwback to the days of feudalism."

I could feel my back stiffening. "What do you mean?"

"He doesn't have to come to London," Martin said. "The whole Yorkshire delegation in the Commons is in his pocket anyway. It doesn't matter if they're Tory or Whig. They simply do as 'my lord' wishes. It's disgraceful."

"It's not so unusual," I said spiritedly. "Look at all these rotten boroughs you're always going on about."

"That's a very different thing. Lord Leyburn hasn't nominated these men. They represent a whole variety of boroughs."

"Then how does he influence them?"

"Feudalism," he grunted, and I smiled.

I found London society a luxurious and lavish world. It was not a world my cousin Martin approved of, and he was quite vocal on the subject of the privileged aristocracy, a class he heartily deplored. I had to agree with many of his strictures; certainly there was outrageous economic inequality in London. One had only to look at the squalid throng of filthy wretches who were to be seen everywhere outside the patrician areas of town to know that. But it seemed to me that it was only in the city that one saw such

sights. There had been no homeless, hungry out-
casts in the Dales of Yorkshire.

The round of social activity went relentlessly
forward. I met a whole collection of young men,
but there were two in particular whom I liked.
One was Lord Stowe. He was tall and thin and
clever-looking and had a wonderful sense of
humor. Grandmama liked him as well, which
meant he must have money as well as a title.
Grandmama was interested in that sort of thing.

The other young man was Lord Henry Sandcroft, a younger son of the Duke of Markham. He
was in the Guards and very serious about a
military career. There was a dedicated quality to
him that was quite formidable. He was quite
different from the other idle men who thronged
London for the Season. I liked him very, very
much. Grandmama, however, tended to be
rather cool toward him. His father might be a
duke, but his financial expectations evidently did
not impress her.

The man I spent the greatest amount of time
with, however, was my cousin Martin. We were
comfortable together. I had never had a brother,
but if I had, I think I would have felt toward him
much as I felt toward Martin.

In early June my grandparents and I attended a
ball at Lady Bridgewater's. It was quite an inter-
national affair as Lord Bridgewater was a power
in the government, and I was standing talking to

a French gentleman when the event happened that would change the color of the world for me. Monseigneur de Varennes lifted his champagne glass to sip it and glanced casually over my head. His hand stilled.

"But who is that?" he asked me. His voice was quite awestruck. I looked.

He was standing at the ballroom door surveying the scene before him with such perfect and natural arrogance that I quite understood Monseigneur de Varennes' awe. So might Lucifer have looked at the legions of hell after the fall.

"That is the Earl of Leyburn," I said out of a constricted throat.

"Leyburn? So. One knows that name, of course."

We watched as Diccon scanned the crowd, sublimely indifferent to the interest he was exciting. He was impeccably dressed in black coat, white waistcoat, and satin knee breeches. Mr. Fitzallan must have gotten him to the tailor after all. His black hair was trimmed shorter than I remembered, but the face was the same.

"*Mais, c'est un grand diable,*" Monseigneur de Varennes breathed beside me. And at that moment Diccon's eyes rested upon me.

"Mademoiselle," said my companion, "I believe he is coming this way."

He was. He crossed the room swiftly with his long individual stride that barely touched the ground, and it was as if a gust of exhilarating air from his own beloved moors blew through the room with him. He stopped directly in front of me, his dark eyes glittering, his lips curled in the pretense of a smile.

"I heard you were in London," he said, and stared at me.

My heart was thundering. "How—how are you, Diccon?" I said weakly, and then flushed at the unconscious familiarity.

The smile became even more sardonic than before. He didn't answer. I could feel my back stiffening.

"May I present the Vicomte de Varennes?" I said with what I hoped was icy politeness.

"How do you do." Diccon barely glanced at him. "You're looking well, Valentine. The London air must agree with you."

"Thank you." I looked up at him and everything inside me seemed to give way. This was the face I loved, the face I called up in the night, the face that haunted me by day. He was furious with me.

"Valentine, I did not know you were acquainted with Lord Leyburn." It was my grandmother.

Diccon turned to look at her. "I was acquainted with Valentine's father," he said blandly. "A splendid chap. You must be Lady Ardsley, ma'am." He smiled.

Grandmama's whole face softened. "Yes, my lord, I am Valentine's grandmother," she replied with dignity.

"I am delighted to see she is being so well looked after." He nodded smoothly and took r·y hand. "Come along and dance, Valentine," and he walked me toward the floor. My grandmother and the Vicomte de Varennes stood and watched us go.

"You little wretch," he said as soon as we were out of hearing range. "Why the hell did you run away like that?"

"I told you why, my lord," I replied with a fair imitation of Grandmama's dignity. "I wrote you a letter."

"You wrote me a lot of nonsense." He sounded savage. "It's lucky for you, my girl, that your grandparents were willing to take you in. You weren't disguised as a boy that time. God knows what could have happened to you."

"I can take care of myself."

He said something extremely unflattering under his breath and I glanced at him. He was beginning to put me out of temper. I had run away solely on his behalf and here he was acting as if I had done something terrible. I should have thought he'd found my disappearance a blessed release.

"You didn't want to marry me," I said fiercely. "Why are you making such a fuss?"

"I have to marry someone," he replied. "It might as well have been you. We get along."

I stared at him, speechless. Then I collected my wits. "You are the most arrogant, bloody-minded *bastard.*" I stopped because he was beginning to smile.

"That's my girl," he said encouragingly. "I was starting to think that all these fine clothes had changed you."

I saw red. He still thought I was a child. Any minute now and he would pat me on the head. I narrowed my eyes and stared up at him. "Did it ever occur to you, my lord, that perhaps *I* might not wish to marry *you?*"

He smiled, the smile that turned all my bones to water. "No," he said simply. He knew too well that I thought he was wonderful. Damnation.

I raised my chin and tried to look dignified. "Well, I've grown up, Diccon. I am nineteen years old now."

He looked thunderstruck. "Nineteen! Good God, you'll be donning a cap before I know it."

I laughed. I didn't want to, but I couldn't help it.

"All your comrades sent their greetings," he continued.

I brightened. "Georgie?"

"Georgie. And Robert. Your companions in crime. I'll wager you haven't had a decent game of dice since you ran away."

I grinned. "I haven't."

"We'll have to see about rectifying that," he said, and then the movements of the dance separated us.

When the set was over, Diccon very properly returned me to my grandmother. When next I saw him, he was dancing with Lady Barbara Bevil. They made a breathtakingly beautiful couple. I felt unutterably depressed.

"So Leyburn decided to put in an appearance." Martin sounded as gloomy as I felt. We watched the black and golden heads on the dance floor for a moment in silence, then he looked at me. "You never told me you knew Leyburn."

"Oh. Well, he was a friend of Papa's," I explained awkwardly.

"I've never seen him before." Martin's face was decidedly glum. "No wonder Barbara waited."

I had suspected for a week or more that my cousin was not disinterested when it came to Lady Barbara Bevil. He always managed a dance with her, and I had several times seen them sitting out a set together. They appeared to spend a great deal of their time arguing.

Lord Henry Sandcroft appeared now at my other elbow. He followed the direction of our eyes and, like us—like half the ballroom, in fact—watched Diccon dance with Lady Barbara. The music came to an end and Diccon escorted his partner back to her mother. Then he moved a little away from the crowd and stood before one of the great windows, head erect, hands clasped behind his back. His very stillness, however, gave a distinct impression of energy, almost of violence.

"There is a man who gives the lie to all of your fine theories, Wakefield," Lord Henry remarked.

"Why is that, Sandcroft?"

"I look at Leyburn and can't help but come to the conclusion that in human beings, as in horses, there is something to be said for the hereditary principle." Lord Henry looked at Martin and smiled.

Martin was staring at Diccon; his mouth looked decidedly grim.

I turned to Lord Henry. "Have you come to claim your dance, Lord Henry?"

"I have," he replied promptly, and led me out to the floor.

16

I didn't see Diccon for four days after Lady
Bridgewater's ball. I couldn't imagine what he
was doing; I found it almost impossible to picture
Diccon in the role of man-about-town. He was
never idle, never self-indulgent, as so many men
of my London acquaintances appeared to be.

He called at Grandmother's one afternoon
while I was out driving with Lord Stowe, and
when I arrived home, it was to find that we had
been invited to a performance of the London
Musical Society the following evening. There
was to be a harpsichord recital.

Grandmama was in high gig. She was not herself at all musical, but evidently an invitation
from the great Lord Leyburn was important

enough for her to submit herself to the boredom of hours of harpsichord.

There was a harpsichord as well as a piano at Carlton Castle, and I knew Diccon played both. I myself had only experience of the piano, but I had always been intrigued by the very different sound of the harpsichord.

I dressed most carefully for the evening. I wanted very much to look grown up and wished heartily that I could wear a low-cut gown of Italian silk instead of the pale and prim and pretty dresses considered suitable to a girl in her first Season. I chose my lowest-cut gown, which wasn't very low at all—not, I thought gloomily, that it would make very much difference—and I put on my shoes with the highest heels. My hair, finally, was looking quite presentable and I had lost last year's tan so my skin was back to its usual creamy color. I surveyed myself critically in the mirror and thought I looked nice.

The recital was being given at the Earl of Oxford's house, and when we arrived, the ballroom had been set up with rows and rows of gilt chairs. The earl, an old man whom I had not met before, greeted us with his sister, Lady Elinor Barnett, beside him. He smiled at me kindly.

"So you are the young lady Leyburn tells me is so fond of Bach. I think you will enjoy our evening very much, my dear."

"I'm sure I shall," I said, and we went into the ballroom to take our seats.

There were very few people present whom I recognized from my frivolous rounds and I was by far the youngest person in attendance. I was looking curiously at the lovely harpsichord standing in the front of the room when Diccon came in and sat down next to me.

"That's a Tashin," he informed me.

"A Tashin?"

"The harpsichord was made by Pascal Tashin, a wonderful harpsichord maker in the French School. Its sound is singularly beautiful. I know." He smiled. "I've been playing it all afternoon."

"Who is going to play this evening?" I asked curiously.

"Pierre Ramatin." He glanced at me. "Just wait," he promised. "You don't know the harpsichord, do you?"

"No."

A very faint smile lingered on his lips. "Wait."

A tall, very thin man came briskly into the ballroom and took his seat at the instrument. There was a brief pause and then he began to play.

He played Bach. For two straight hours he played Bach, a Bach I had never heard before. The harpsichord had a very different sound from the piano: more austere, highly distinctive, extremely complex. He played the "Chromatic Fantasy and Fugue," a piece I had often played on the piano, but the sound and the shape were completely different.

I sat and listened, aware only of the music and of the happiness of being in the company of someone who felt as I did. Bach had never been more awesome. I could hear all the profound intricacies, the overlapping melodies. The music and I were perfectly attuned. I sat without breathing, it seemed, and so did Diccon.

When the last note had died away, there was a moment of perfect silence before the clapping began. I turned to look at Diccon and he looked back at me, quite gravely, and nodded.

"Thank heavens that is over," my grandmother murmured from my other side.

Diccon smiled very faintly and his hand just touched mine. He leaned across me and said, "There are refreshments in the saloon, Lady Ardsley. May I bring you some champagne punch?"

He escorted us to the supper room and saw Grandmama comfortably ensconced with some punch and some lobster patties. He then very thoughtfully provided her with an elderly conversation partner, Lord Bocking, whom she apparently knew quite well, and took me away to see the harpsichord.

I was fingering the keys and listening to Diccon when M. Ramatin appeared at our side. He looked at Diccon.

"Please play, my lord," he said quietly.

Diccon shrugged. "It is too late."

The other man was regarding him very seriously. "I have heard of you, of course. Please, you will not deny me the opportunity of hearing you play?"

Without another word, Diccon sat down. "What do you want to hear?"

"What Lord Oxford tells me you were playing this afternoon?"

Diccon raised a black eyebrow.

"I beg you," the man said.

Diccon raised his hands and began to play from the Goldberg Variations. I sat down in a gilt chair and M. Ramatin sat beside me. I had once attempted the Goldberg Variations on the piano. They are perhaps the most difficult single keyboard work ever written.

Diccon played for half an hour and when he had finished, the ballroom was almost full again.

"How long have you been practicing that, my lord?" It was M. Ramatin.

Diccon looked surprised. "This afternoon," he said. "I thought Oxford told you that."

"I mean," said M. Ramatin sternly, "for how long *before* this afternoon?"

"Oh," said Diccon easily, "I haven't played any of the Goldberg in years."

M. Ramatin stared at him in wonder, shook his head, and walked away.

"The poor man is awestruck," I said with amusement.

"He is a very fine musician." Diccon was serious. "I want to get him to come to Carlton. Excuse me for a moment, Valentine, will you?" He went off in pursuit of M. Ramatin and I turned to find my grandmother at my side.

"We are leaving, Valentine. I cannot endure to sit through another hour of this."

I sighed. She had really been very patient. "All right, Grandmama." We got our cloaks and left before I could speak again to Diccon.

I went for a ride in the park the following morning with my cousin Martin and we met Diccon galloping along Rotten Row to the obvious displeasure of several other riders. One did not gallop in Hyde Park. One cantered, decorously.

Diccon pulled up when he saw me and I introduced him to Martin.

"That's a new horse," I said, and looked admiringly at Diccon's gray. The horse wanted to gallop, but Diccon held him relentlessly to a walk.

"He's Newcastle's," Diccon informed me. "I didn't want to bring my own cattle all the way to London. Newcastle has been having a difficult time with this gray, so I volunteered to teach him some manners."

I looked up at him, at his black hair disheveled from the run, his brilliant dark eyes, his flawlessly proud profile. I laughed. "What manners? You've been tearing up and down the park like a maniac."

"That was a reward," he returned imperturbably. "He walked over here like a gentleman."

"Perhaps you did not realize it, my lord, but it is not the thing to gallop in the park at this hour." Martin sounded stiff and disapproving, and Diccon turned his head to stare at him.

"Wakefield. Are you the fellow who is going to inherit from Ardsley?"

"Yes."

"Ah." Diccon looked him up and down, and Martin's back got noticeably stiffer. "Well, Wakefield," his lordship went on in the pleasant voice that always made me nervous, "I find I am not interested in what is the thing to do."

Martin's chin looked remarkably stubborn. "I might have expected as much," he said grimly.

Diccon's face lit with a charming and thoroughly untrustworthy smile. "Certainly you might."

Martin began to look really angry. I knew what

was wrong with him, and it had nothing to do with Diccon's galloping his horse in the park. I gave his lordship a minatory look and said, "I enjoyed the music last night very much. Thank you for inviting me."

"You're quite welcome," he said mockingly.

"Don't let us keep you from your lesson." I smiled sunnily and glanced at Martin from the corner of my eye. His hands on the reins looked rigid. Diccon was provoking him just by being there.

"Good-bye," I said firmly, and after a minute he laughed.

"Good-bye, sweetheart. I'll see you this evening."

He was off in an abrupt flash of silver gray, and I turned to find Martin looking at me in astonishment.

"Sweetheart?" he said.

Damn Diccon. He had done that on purpose.

"Lord Leyburn was a very good friend of Papa's," I said. "What is on the cards for tonight?"

"A reception at Carlton House."

My jaw dropped. *"Carlton* House? Can Diccon really be going there?"

"Diccon?" echoed Martin in even greater astonishment than before.

"Come along, Martin," I said impatiently, "let's canter." I started up the row at a pace that was scarcely decorous.

17

Carlton House was the residence of the king's eldest son, the Prince of Wales. The prince had assumed great political importance because of the uncertain sanity of his father, George III. There was every likelihood of the prince becoming Prince Regent within a very short time and the government would depend upon whom he sent for to head it. The Tories under Spencer Perceval were presently in power, but the Whigs had long enjoyed the favor of the Prince of Wales and so they hoped that their chance was close at hand.

I received all of this political background from my cousin Martin during the remainder of our morning ride.

"The Whigs were in for a short time after Pitt died, but when we lost Fox, everything went to pieces. The Tories came back again under Portland. When Canning and Castlereagh had that ridiculous duel, they all had to resign and things looked hopeful for us, but the king brought in Perceval and he seems pretty well entrenched. Our best hope lies in Prinny."

"What you are saying, then, is that everyone is buttering up the Prince of Wales."

He smiled ruefully. "That is what I am saying, Valentine. And that is why all the world will be at Carlton House tonight. The prince has made no commitments as yet. He is as pleasant to his father's ministers as he is to his old friends of the opposition."

"Will it really make any difference to the country who gets in?" I asked.

He stared at me, aghast. "Of course it will, Valentine. With the Whigs we will have some progress at least."

"Oh. Progress. I often wonder if it is all it's cracked up to be."

He looked at me with injured dignity and said nothing. Evidently he did not consider my remark worthy of a reply.

In the afternoon I went for a drive in the park with Lord Henry Sandcroft. A great part of one's day in London revolved around Hyde Park. It was frightfully tame.

Lord Henry and I discussed the latest news from the Peninsula. The Spanish army had been defeated, but Wellington was in Portugal waiting to begin a new campaign.

"I have some news for you, Valentine," he said after a little silence had fallen. "I shall be going out myself. It's all settled. I've been appointed to Wellington's staff."

"Harry, how splendid." I smiled. He had wanted this appointment for quite some time.

"My mother doesn't think so," he replied a little dryly.

"Mothers don't like to see their little boys go to war."

"I'm not a little boy." His voice was even dryer than before, and I looked up at him. He was an extremely well-built young man with a strong aquiline nose and a quite decided chin. He was twenty-five and most certainly not a child.

"I know," I said placatingly, "but mothers don't think that way."

"She's afraid I'll get killed."

"Well, you might. Men do get killed in war."

He gave me a very strange look. "You don't sound very upset by the prospect."

"Everyone has to die sometime, Harry. The thing to do is to live, to be happy, and not to worry oneself unduly about the way one goes out." I smiled at him. "I should be very unhappy to hear of your death. But I would never want to stop you from doing what you felt you had to do."

There was a pause. His eyes were focused straight ahead, between his horse's ears. Then he spoke, still without looking at me. "I don't believe you would."

"It's because you *are* a man," I explained. "Some people need to be taken care of. You don't."

"Nor do you." He turned to look at me at last. "And the amazing thing is, you don't even realize how extraordinary you are."

Martin had said all the world would be at Carlton House, and it appeared he was right. The graceful double staircase that went up to the Chinese Room was jammed with people. The prince was graciously greeting his guests and I curtsied deeply when Grandmama presented me.

All the rooms were crowded, with people and with objects both. There were displays of Sevres china and collections of clocks and mirrors and bronzes. The entire effect was overpowering. I was standing looking at a marble bust by Coysevox when a pleasant voice spoke next to me.

"Do you admire sculpture?"

I turned to find a nice-looking man with brown hair and sophisticated gray eyes watching me. Grandmama was talking to someone at a little distance and not paying attention to me.

"Busts are not my favorite," I admitted.

The man raised an eyebrow. "You don't admire the prince's taste?"

"I did not say that. I have never seen such an extensive collection of beautiful things."

"You fit in among them very well. I've been out of town this last month and I must confess I do not know your name."

"I'm Valentine Langley. Lord Ardsley is my grandfather."

His other eyebrow went up. "Ah. Yes. Miss Langley."

"How do you do. And you are?"

He smiled faintly. "My name is Brummell."

So this was the famous Beau Brummell, the arbiter of all fashion, the man whose approval could raise a nonentity to social heights and whose disapproval could banish one to the nether depths of the country. I smiled at him and said nothing. He was the one who had started the conversation.

"It was too bad of you to have sneaked in upon the *ton* in my absence, Miss Langley," he said.

"It was a dreadful mistake," I replied

immediately. "We were not properly informed of your schedule."

"You see, it is my duty to put a seal of acceptability on all new members of society," he explained gently.

"I do hope you approve of me, Mr. Brummell." Actually, I cared not the snap of my fingers about his feelings one way or another, but I always try to be polite.

There was a glimmer of amusement in his gray eyes. "I understand you rejected Lawton. That is a recommendation."

The Marquis of Lawton was a very stuffy, very pompous, very noble, very rich young man who used to ask me to dance rather frequently. I had taken to telling him my card was all filled. He was a dreadful bore.

"Lord Lawton was never interested in me, Mr. Brummell," I said firmly. "I believe he likes Lady Barbara Bevil."

"I see." He looked even more amused, and Grandmama appeared at his shoulder. She looked a little apprehensive.

"Grandmama, may I present Mr. Brummell," I said dutifully.

The two of them made all the appropriate murmurs, then Grandmama said, "I did not know you were acquainted with my granddaughter, Mr. Brummell."

"I took the liberty of introducing myself, ma'am," he replied smoothly. "I have heard a great deal about Miss Langley since I returned to London."

Poor Grandmama looked distinctly nervous. It was really too bad of him to upset her.

"All of it good, I'm sure," I said sternly, and gave him a quelling look.

His lips twitched. "Assuredly."

Grandmama brightened noticeably.

"I should hope so," I said, and Mr. Brummell laughed.

There was a stir at the door and I looked up to see that Diccon was coming in. He was dressed in black evening clothes and his black hair was brushed and smooth on his arrogantly held head. He looked like an angel in mortal dress.

"Leyburn." It was the Prince of Wales' voice. He beamed at Diccon, his whole well-corseted person excuding good humor. "My dear fellow, this is a great pleasure."

Diccon was in front of him now, and from my place across the room I could see how he stiffened. He did not like fat German princes being genial with him. It was an almost imperceptible movement, but I saw it, and His Royal Highness must have, too. He held out his hand and said with dignity, "You are welcome to Carlton House."

There was a moment of silence in the room as Diccon regarded his future sovereign. No doubt he was thinking of how the Fitzallans had been making and breaking kings while the Hanovers were still petty German electors. Then he took the outstretched hand and bowed, very slightly.

"Thank you, Your Highness," he said gravely, a prince talking to a prince. "It is a pleasure to be here."

Diccon spent the first hour of his visit talking to a great variety of gentlemen and to Lady Barbara Bevil. Martin and I, depressed by the sight of the two of them together, escaped to the conservatory. The Carlton House conservatory was like no other of its kind. It was a cathedral, with Gothic pillars, tessellated ceilings, and a marble floor. Martin and I sat down on a bench next to a collection of strange-looking cacti and regarded each other gloomily.

"Where's Sandcroft?" he asked me moodily. "Stowe's had a clear field with you tonight."

"He was on duty," I said. "He's finally got his posting to the Peninsula."

"Good for **him**."

"Yes."

"Here they are, hiding behind the cacti," said a familiar voice, and Diccon came into sight around a huge azalea. Right after him came Lady Barbara Bevil. Martin jumped to his feet.

"Valentine," said Diccon charmingly. "I don't believe you've met Lady Barbara. As you've been sharing the same dancing partners all Season, I thought you girls ought to be formally introduced."

"How do you do, Lady Barbara," I said politely. Up close she was even more beautiful than I had thought. Her eyes were the color of sapphires. Mine, alas, are quite dark, more gray than blue. I looked at her beautiful face and hated her.

Lady Barbara was looking at Martin. "Where have you been hiding yourself all evening, Mr. Wakefield?" she asked sweetly.

"I have been talking politics with Brougham," he replied with dignity.

"It seems to be quite a political evening," Diccon remarked. "I was cornered for half an hour by Liverpool and Sidmouth."

Martin looked scornful. "Hah," he said. "Two of the rankest bigots in London."

"They are friends of my papa," said Lady Barbara.

Martin looked even more scornful. "I know."

"My cousin is a reformer, my lord," I explained to Diccon. "A radical, if you will. He doesn't approve of the old ways and is in favor of progress."

"Is he, by God?" Diccon looked at Martin with great skepticism. "What precisely are you in favor of, Mr. Wakefield?"

"Parliamentary reform," said Martin vigorously. "Universal suffrage; the secret ballot; more frequent general elections and an end to rotten boroughs and corruption at Westminster."

"And what do you think all that will accomplish, Mr. Wakefield?" It was Lady Barbara.

"Greater equality among Englishmen," Martin said stoutly.

Diccon's eyes on Martin's face were level and enigmatic. "What I think, Mr. Wakefield, is that if all you radical gentlemen stayed home and looked after your own land and your own people, we would see far more prosperity and equality in this country. When I think of progress I think of the factories of Leeds and of Bradford. There isn't a tenant of mine in the Dales who isn't better off than the poor wretches toiling in the cities under the shadow of progress."

"People are being forced off the land, Lord Leyburn."

"They are not being forced off *my* land," Diccon returned implacably.

"You," said Martin with flashing eyes, "you run your own little kingdom up there in Yorkshire."

"You're damn right I do."

"You are medieval, my lord."

"I am honest," returned Diccon pleasantly. I

163

knew that tone of voice and waited for the dagger. "I don't go about spouting progressive ideas that make me feel moral without damaging my position."

Martin's back was ramrod straight. "Just what do you mean by that, my lord?"

"I mean that I haven't heard anything about your renouncing your inheritance. You will be Lord Ardsley one day, will you not?"

"Are you accusing Mr. Wakefield of insincerity, Lord Leyburn?" asked Lady Barbara.

"I'm quite certain that Mr. Wakefield wants to *feel* sincere, Lady Barbara. But it seems as if all his ideas are theories only. It's a sort of amusement, I suppose. People in London spend a great deal of thought and time and money on amusement." Diccon spoke with a kind of cool detachment that was belied by the flicker of temper I saw in his eyes.

Without another word, Martin turned on his heel and left us.

"You were very rude, my lord," said Lady Barbara reproachfully.

Diccon shrugged. "I see he's lighted under the tropical hanging plants. I think you'd better go hold his hand, Lady Barbara. He might be about to cry."

She gave him an uncertain look but walked off after Martin. Diccon turned to me.

"Are you going to insult me as well?" I asked affably.

"I might. What an insufferable prig that fellow is."

"He is not," I returned. "He is very nice and he is sincere."

Diccon raised an incredulous eyebrow. "Don't tell me you've fallen for that pap?"

"Not exactly." I sighed. "Martin is truly in earnest about reform, Diccon. But I see your point too. He seems to want to do away with a good many things, but he seems to want to stay himself. I suppose that's natural, but it is rather inconsistent."

His face relaxed a little. "I have no patience with a fellow like that," he informed me unnecessarily. "He will inherit a position of great responsibility and he's all in a muddle about himself, his position, his power—about everything, in fact."

"I like him," I said stubbornly. "He may be a muddle, but he's a very nice muddle."

"Is he?" There was a strange stillness about Diccon suddenly as he looked at me. I looked back inquiringly, and another face appeared from behind the azaleas.

"There you are, Miss Langley. Lady Ardsley asked me to find you and escort you into supper."

It was the narrow, clever, humorous face of Lord Stowe. I put my hand on his arm, nodded to Diccon, and allowed Lord Stowe to escort me to the supper room.

Martin and Lady Barbara were before me, sitting together under the displeased eye of the duchess, Barbara's mother. Fifteen minutes later Diccon came in with a smoldering-looking brunette. They appeared to be absorbed in each other and I found I hated the unknown lady quite as much as I hated Lady Barbara. I was very glad when it was time to go home.

18

Every Season the Marchioness of Ravensworth
had a garden party at her home on the Thames
and All the Best People attended. My grandparents, though long absent from society, were
definitely Best Persons and so we were all
invited to this annual alfresco affair. Borrow
House was only a few miles outside of London
and the day was delightfully sunny and warm. I
wished I could spend the afternoon hacking a
horse over the countryside instead of making
conversation at a large party.

I didn't know if Diccon would be there. I
didn't know if I wanted him to be there. I was in
a worse muddle than Martin, I thought gloomily.

Borrow House was right on the river, and the

gardens and the views were indeed beautiful. I strolled around with Grandpapa for a while, meeting and talking to a great variety of people. Then Lord Stowe came up to me and Grandpapa was hailed by one of his old cronies.

"Lord Stowe is going to show me the rose garden, Grandpapa," I said, and he smiled and nodded, delighted to get me off his hands so he could settle down to a long gossip with General Rawley.

"I've been looking for you for an hour, Miss Langley," Lord Stowe said as we strolled off together. "I was at the theater last night and the most hilarious thing happened."

I looked up at him expectantly. He was one of the funniest people I had ever met. "Tell me," I demanded.

He did. It was a long story that involved a Romeo who forgot his lines and a Juliet who had tripped and nearly fallen off her balcony. It was not so much what had happened as the way he told it that was so funny. I laughed so hard there were tears in my eyes.

We came out of the path and into the rose garden, and the first thing I saw as I looked around me was Diccon. Lord Stowe and I were still gurgling with hilarity.

"Valentine," said Diccon, and nodded. He was not smiling.

I gave a joyous gulp and tried to compose myself. "Good afternoon, my lord." I caught a movement out of the corner of my eye and the sultry brunette of Carlton House made a sudden appearance.

"I'm Leyburn," Diccon was saying to Lord Stowe.

"Stowe," the young man replied with dignity. The two men looked at each other and I looked at the brunette. She was disgustingly voluptuous. No one made any attempt to introduce me.

"How do you do," I said to the woman who was now standing next to Diccon. "I'm Valentine Langley." I forced myself to smile.

"May I introduce the Vicomtese Kirkton," said Diccon. He looked annoyed.

The vicomtesse and I made polite noises, and then Lord Stowe said, "We must go find your grandmother, Miss Langley. She will be looking for you."

"Yes," I said. I nodded as haughtily as I could manage to the vicomtesse and barely glanced at Diccon. I smiled up at Lord Stowe and we walked back down the path we had come along. But all the time, as I laughed and chatted with my escort, I saw only one thing in my mind's eye: the vicomtesse's face as she had looked quickly at Diccon just before we left. No woman's eyes had ever said more plainly, "I am one of your possessions." I felt unutterably bleak. Lord Stowe was talking on and on about his mother and how she wished to meet me, and I nodded and smiled and listened with less than half my attention.

We found Grandmama, and Lord Stowe exerted himself to please her, for which I was very grateful. I was not feeling very sprightly myself.

We were sitting on one of the benches sipping iced punch when Martin appeared. His face looked as bleak as I felt. When he proposed taking me out in a boat on the river, I agreed promptly. There is a great deal of truth to the proverb that misery loves company.

We were drifting along in one of Lady Ravensworth's little rowboats when I said to him, "Did you and Lady Barbara quarrel?"

He looked startled. "How did you know?"

"I'm not blind, Martin. Or stupid. I know you love her. And I know she is not uninterested in you."

He rested his arms on the oars and regarded me drearily. "She says she loves me. But she won't marry me, Val."

"Why not?"

"Her father doesn't approve of me. He says I'm a radical. He wants her to marry Leyburn."

"You *are* a radical," I pointed out.

"Yes." He looked fierce. "And I cannot change my political views—not even for Barbara."

"Good for you, Martin," I said approvingly.

"I don't feel very good," he mumbled.

"I know." I reached over and covered his hand briefly with mine. "Does—does Lady Barbara want to marry Lord Leyburn?"

"No. He frightens her, I think. But she is very much under her father's influence. And he is set on the Leyburn alliance."

"Has Lord Leyburn proposed?"

"No, thank God. He's a slippery devil and proud as Lucifer. Who knows what he'll do."

"Hmph. He seems to be spending a great deal of time with Lady Kirkton."

He raised an eyebrow. "Oh, but he's not about to marry *her*, Val."

"Why not?"

"It's not necessary," he said.

I remembered the look on Lady Kirkton's face and knew exactly what Martin meant.

"Well, I think it's too bad of Lady Barbara to want you to change your convictions," I said bracingly. "And I think she is an idiot to allow her father to dictate to her whom she is to marry. She is the one who has to live with the man, after all. Not her father."

"Barbara isn't spineless, Val," he protested.

"She sounds it. I certainly wouldn't let anyone marry me off to someone I didn't care for."

He was watching me with a small smile on his handsome fresh-skinned face. "I know that," he said. "I doubt anyone could have moved you to do anything you didn't want to do at age nine, never mind at nineteen."

He was probably right. My father had expressed himself similarly on a variety of occasions.

"Are you quite certain the duke doesn't like you?" I asked Martin.

"He thinks I'm poison."

"Well, then, Lady Barbara will have to elope with you."

"You've lost your mind, Val. Barbara would never do such a thing."

"You said she loved you."

"She says she does." His gray eyes were very bright. "I know she does. She'd marry me in a minute if her father agreed. She doesn't really care about my politics. It's the duke."

"Then eloping is the only way." He opened his mouth to protest again, but I went on relentlessly. "Martin, do you or don't you want to marry that girl?"

"Of course I do."

"Then stop being such a mule and help me think of some scheme that will persuade her to elope with you."

He looked scandalized. "Do you mean compromise her?"

"No." I frowned. "There must be some way to shake her composure, Martin. One of the problems is that she's too sure of you. You hover about her like a half-starved wolf."

"Val." He reached forward and took both my hands in his. "You marvelous wonderful girl. That's it. I need to make Barbara jealous."

I smiled with pleasure. "Of course. That's just what you must do. But with whom?"

He beamed at me and raised one of my hands to his lips. "With you, Valentine, my darling. With you."

19

Martin docked our boat and helped me out with great solicitude. I bit my lip and tried not to giggle. When we were walking up the lawn, he took my arm and bent his head to murmur in my ear.

"We are being glared at from three different directions."

I gazed up at him soulfully—at least I thought it was soulfully. In general, soulfulness is not just my style.

"Three?" I inquired.

"Barbara is standing with Leyburn pretending not to notice us. But she does." Martin sounded very smug. "And your two swains are looking daggers at me. I only hope this doesn't end in one or both of them calling me out."

"Don't go," I advised, and batted my eyelashes.

He grinned. "I won't. At least not with Sandcroft. He'd make mincemeat of me."

"May I escort you back to your grandmother, Valentine? I believe she is desirous of your company."

"Why, yes." I glanced quickly up at Diccon's face and then to Lady Barbara's. There was a very faint line between her beautiful brows. Good. "Why don't you show Lady Barbara the rose garden, Martin?" I continued. "I'll see you tomorrow for our drive in the park."

He gave me a very sweet smile. If he smiled like that at Lady Barbara, I didn't see how she could resist him.

"Till tomorrow, Val," he said, and we looked quickly away from each other before we burst into laughter. He moved off with Barbara and I turned to Diccon.

"You are behaving like a trollop," he said to me coldly.

"What!"

"You heard me. Holding hands with that meretricious radical in full view of the entire population of this bloody garden party."

"There is no need for you to swear," I said with great dignity. "And speaking of trollops, where is your friend Lady Kirkton?"

"Don't be impertinent." He spoke coolly, but

there was something menacing in his rigidly controlled voice.

"I'm not the one who initiated this conversation," I snapped. "And what is more, it is no concern of yours who I speak to or who I choose to hold hands with. I don't work for you any longer, Lord Leyburn."

He stared down at me for a long silent minute, his mouth bitter and ruthless. I could feel my heart hammering. I wanted to lean my body against his, to hold him close to me. I wanted to love him, not to fight him. But he still thought of me as a reckless child.

"There you are, Miss Langley," said a voice at my elbow. "I have been looking for you this past hour." It was Lord Henry Sandcroft.

"Well, you've found me," I said with an effort at lightness. "Lord Leyburn, do you know Lord Henry Sandcroft?"

"No." After a pause Diccon held out his hand. "You're Markham's son, aren't you?"

Lord Henry shook hands. "Yes."

"Lord Henry is going out to the Peninsula in a few weeks," I informed Diccon. "He's got an appointment to Wellington's staff."

For the first time all afternoon I saw Diccon smile. "Congratulations."

"Thank you, my lord." Lord Henry's determined-looking face softened slightly under the radiance of that smile. "It's been a great bore this last year, hanging about London."

"I know." A shadow crossed Diccon's face. "I always feel like a trapped animal in London. And then one gets involved in affairs like this"—he waved his hand to encompass the gardens and the people—"doing the polite to people one wouldn't entertain in one's woodshed at home."

Lord Henry grinned. "I know what you mean."

"Well, at least the two of you can escape," I said. "I'm the one who is stuck here."

"If you marry a Parliamentary chap you certainly will be," said Lord Henry.

It took me a minute to realize he was talking about Martin. I thought it prudent to remain silent.

"Let me show you the summerhouse, Miss Langley," Lord Henry said coaxingly. "I've scarcely seen you in days and I've something of great importance to say to you."

"Grandmama is looking for me, Henry."

"No, she's not. She was gossiping away with Lady Witton only a few minutes ago."

I looked up at Diccon.

"Lady Ardsley desired me to bring Valentine to her," he said, and gave me a smile of such beauty that even Lord Henry was awed. I knew that smile and I knew he was lying.

"I am quite certain Grandmama will not wish me to interrupt her conversation with Lady Witton," I said austerely to that angel's face. His dark eyes narrowed slightly and I started back, refusing to be browbeaten. For some reason, he did not want me to go off with Lord Henry.

"Will you come for a walk with me, Valentine?" Lord Henry sounded very grave.

I tore my eyes away from Diccon's face and looked up at him. I put my hand on his arm and smiled. "Of course I will, Harry."

Without another word, Diccon turned on his heel and strode off. I stared after him for a minute as he walked across the lawn, at his arrogant head and long free stride. Heads turned all along the way to watch his exit. Then I turned with Lord Henry in the opposite direction and walked toward the summerhouse.

There were two other couples in the summerhouse when we got there, and Lord Henry swore under his breath.

"Why don't we walk along the path," I said soothingly, and he nodded and turned toward the gate I had indicated. We let ourselves into a little wood and walked for a few minutes in silence. I was preoccupied with thoughts of Diccon and jumped a little when Harry began to speak.

"I leave for Lisbon in two weeks," he told me.

"I must go down to Markham tomorrow to spend some time. Mama will be very upset if I leave without saying good-bye."

"Of course you must go to Markham," I agreed. "Two weeks!" I looked up at his tough, aquiline profile and felt a pang. I liked Harry very much. "I shall miss you," I said.

He stopped and looked down at me. "I've wanted this post ever since Wellington went out there," he said somberly. "I've wrecked my mother's peace to get it. And now I find that I don't want to go." He picked up my hands and held them tightly. "I don't want to leave you, Valentine."

"Oh," I said.

"I never planned to marry," he went on tensely. "Not for years and years, at least. I have ambition. But I never thought I would find a girl like you."

"I'm not so special, Harry," I said lamely.

"Oh, Valentine." It was a cry almost of pain, and he pulled me into his arms and held me close. I rested my cheek against his shoulder and felt his strong, hard young body pressed to mine.

"Will you marry me?" His lips were buried in my hair and his voice sounded a little muffled. "Will you come out to Lisbon with me, Valentine? I have no right to ask it of you, I know. But will you?"

"You have every right to ask me, Harry. And of all the men I have met in London, you are the one I could have loved."

After a moment his arms around me loosened. "Could have?"

"Yes," I said sadly, and stepped back from him. I picked up his hand and looked at the strong broad fingers. "Perhaps I shall marry someday. But you would not be satisfied with what I have to give, Harry. Other men might be, but not you." Still holding his hand, I looked up into his face. "My heart is already pledged," I said softly.

"Who is it?" he asked.

"Leyburn."

He looked suddenly very bleak. "Leyburn," he repeated. "How can any ordinary man hope to compete with that?"

"You are not an ordinary man."

He gave a short staccato laugh. "How do you know him, Valentine?"

I told him. I told him the whole story. When I had finished, there was a small, bitter smile on his face. But all he said, quietly, was, "I see." Then he took my face between his hands and turned it up.

"Only you," he said.

"Only I would be cork-brained enough to embark on such a scheme," I admitted ruefully.

"That, of course." He smiled more naturally. "And only you would have told me."

"You deserve to know. And I never had a great deal of pride."

"You are the proudest person I have ever known."

I stared at him in astonishment. "I?"

"You. You are Valentine Langley and you don't care in the least what other people may think of you. I have never met anyone less concerned about the opinion of others."

"You should know Diccon," I said.

He still smiled, although his eyes were grave. "Listen to me, Valentine." He ran a gentle finger over my cheekbone. "I love you very much. If ever, at any time, you change your mind and decide to marry me, just write."

I could feel the tears welling up in my eyes and I made no attempt to blink them back.

"I love you too, Harry. But—but not in the way you want me to."

He bent and kissed the drops on my cheeks. "Come," he said. "I'll take you to your grandmother."

20

I felt very cast down the day after the garden party. It distressed me that I had hurt Harry. It distressed me that I could not return his love. There was only unhappiness for me in the love I had chosen. But then, I had not really chosen it; it had chosen me.

Grandmama and I were sitting dully at home with a fire to take the damp out of a chill gray day when Martin arrived at Ardsley House in the late afternoon. He accepted a cup of tea from Grandmama.

"It's going to rain," he told us unnecessarily.

"Yes. It was fortunate that Lady Ravensworth had her garden party yesterday," Grandmama replied.

"What have you been doing all day?" I asked him, more for something to say than because I cared. I was not in a good temper.

Martin put down his cup. "I almost saw a duel this afternoon." He saw he had our complete attention and smiled with satisfaction.

"Well, it wasn't precisely a duel since it took place at Angelo's and the swords were tipped" —Angelo's was a well-known fencing establishment in St. James's Street—"but, by Jupiter, it was the prettiest swordplay I've ever seen. And they were serious—if they weren't surrounded by an audience, I believe they would have gone at it in earnest."

"Who?" Grandmama demanded.

"Why?" I asked.

Martin answered my question first. "You won't believe it," he said in wonder, "but the fight was over King Richard the Third." And so of course I knew who one of the parties was.

"Who was Lord Leyburn fighting?" I asked Martin resignedly.

"Hollingwood."

"Good heavens. I believe Harry once told me he was the premier swordsman in London."

"He was," answered Martin, with emphasis on the past tense. He shook his head. "Leyburn is unbelievable."

"He feels very strongly about Richard the Third," I replied absently.

"Richard the Third?" echoed Grandmama in utter bewilderment. "Isn't he the king who murdered the little princes in the tower?"

"He did not!"

"All right, Val," Martin said soothingly. "We don't want any swords in here."

"Very funny," I said nastily. It really was infuriating how no one cared to learn the truth about Richard.

"I'll tell you what, though," Martin was saying soberly, "Leyburn hasn't made many friends in London."

"Why not?" I demanded.

"Well, this morning, for example. There was no need for him to fly up into the boughs about Hollingworth's perfectly harmless remark."

"I am quite certain that Diccon didn't immediately whip out his sword."

"No. Well. But who really cares about someone whose been dead for centuries?"

"Diccon does. I do." I glared at him. "Do you realize that the little princes were most probably perfectly safe and healthy when the Tower was turned over to Henry the Seventh?"

Martin was putting up his hands. "All right, Val. All right! Richard the Third was a saint. Don't flash your eyes at me."

"What I do not understand, Valentine, is why you should be referring to Lord Leyburn by his given name. Or why his interests and feelings appear to be so well-known to you." Grand-mama had found a topic of far greater interest to her than the last Plantagenet king.

"I'm sorry, Grandmama."

"It is extremely improper."

"I beg your pardon, Grandmama."

"Is there something between you and Lord Leyburn that I am unaware of?"

"Of course not." I spoke quite definitely. "He was a friend of Papa's. That is all."

She gave me a long hard look. "I have never understood how your father came to have a friend of such great eminence."

I narrowed my eyes and looked back at her even harder. "But then, Grandmama, you have never appreciated Papa."

Silence. Checkmate.

Martin cleared his throat. "Are you going to the Brooks' dinner tomorrow, Aunt Mary?"

"Yes, Martin, we are." Grandmama spoke with all her old dignity. "Shall we see you there?"

"Yes."

Grandmama looked at me and smiled compla-cently. Brooks House was not the sort of place one would normally find Martin. Lord Brooks was a die-hard Tory. Poor Grandmama thought Martin was going because I was. He was going, of course, because Barbara would be there. My cousin and I exchanged an amused glance, and

Martin got up to take his leave, promising to see us the following evening.

"I do believe Martin is finally growing up," Grandmama said after he had left. "You know, Valentine, he is quite fond of you."

The poor old dear. I gave her a warm kiss and a hug. She was going to be so disappointed.

Diccon was at the Brooks House dinner. He was the first person I saw when we walked into the drawing room. He was talking to the Duke of Cartington, and as I looked at him, I understood why so many men I knew expressed hostility toward him. It must be difficult for the ordinary man to forgive Diccon for being Diccon.

His dark eyes met mine across the room and for a brief moment I had the strangest feeling that we were alone. Then Grandpapa said something to me and the spell was broken.

Diccon was seated next to Lady Barbara at dinner and I had Lord Stowe on one side of me and Martin on the other. Martin tried to monopolize my attention so as to provoke Barbara. Lord Stowe kept cutting into Martin's conversation, however, and interspersed his remarks to me with some decidedly nasty asides to my cousin. I felt rather like a bone in the middle of a dog fight. I was very glad when dinner was over and the ladies withdrew to the drawing room, leaving the gentlemen to their port.

There was a lovely piano in the drawing room and Lady Brooks asked if one of the ladies would play. The Duchess of Cartington immediately volunteered Barbara. After a little show of bashfulness, she complied.

She played like a stick. She knew all the notes and made no mistakes. Her timing was faultless. But there wasn't an ounce of feeling in her music. It was as abstract and as emotionless as a mathematical formula.

Barbara was still playing when the gentlemen joined us. When she finished, Martin led the raves. His face was actually glowing. He thought she was so wonderful. Poor deluded Martin.

Diccon and I exchanged a glance. No one who played like that could have the slightest feeling for music.

Barbara certainly looked beautiful, though. One had to give her that. Her golden curls were glorious, her eyes as blue as cornflowers. She smiled briefly at Martin and for a moment she was radiant. Martin had been right: she did love him. What a fool she was not to marry him.

"I wonder if we might prevail upon Lord Leyburn to favor us with a piece." It was Lord Brooks, and suddenly I knew where I had seen him before. He had been at the Musical Society harpsichord concert.

"Lord Leyburn?" said one of the gentlemen in

surprise. It was usually the ladies who entertained after dinner.

"Yes," said Lord Brooks. "Please, my lord."

With a slight shrug, Diccon sat down before the piano. There was a moment of expectant silence and then he began to play.

He gave us the "Moonlight Sonata," and as I listened to the achingly beautiful music of Beethoven, I felt such an anguish, such a longing in my heart. I watched Diccon's profile, and my heart cried out to him.

There was absolute silence as Diccon finished. Even Lady Barbara appeared slightly moved by the music. Diccon looked up from the keys at me.

"You next, Miss Langley," he said.

I opened my mouth to protest. I wouldn't have minded following Lady Barbara, but to expect me to play after him!

"Yes, Miss Langley," said Lord Brooks. "We would be honored."

"I don't play like his lordship," I protested faintly.

"Only a handful of people in the world play like his lordship. We understand that perfectly."

"Do play, Valentine," said Grandmama. "She practices for hours every day," she went on to inform Lord Brooks. "I believe she is every bit as good as Lord Leyburn."

I restrained myself from looking heavenward

and went over to the piano. They had asked for it, I thought, and launched with reckless abandon into Beethoven's "Sonata Appassionata." I had only been working on it for a short while, but at the moment it expressed my feelings perfectly.

When I had finished, I stared at Diccon a little defiantly. At least no one could accuse me of playing without passion, like Barbara. His dark eyes were partly screened by half-lowered lashes and we exchanged a look that was strangely unfathomable.

"You are perhaps lacking the technical brilliance of his lordship, Miss Langley," came Lord Brooks' voice, "but you play marvelously. I wonder if you would come one afternoon and play for me?"

His kindly eyes were smiling at me. "I should love to," I said.

"What about some singing?" proposed the duchess, and it turned out that Barbara had a lovely voice. She sang us two songs in her sweet soprano, and then Martin, who had quite a decent baritone, joined her for a duet. They sang very well together.

"Why doesn't Lord Leyburn join you in a duet, Barbara?" the duchess asked. I don't think she was delighted by the sight of her daughter and Martin.

"It's time we heard from Miss Langley as well," said Lord Brooks.

I could feel myself flushing. I have quite a deep voice for a girl, and I had never had singing lessons.

"Come, Miss Langley, and sing something with me," said Diccon. His dark eyes were laughing at me and I rose reluctantly from my chair and went to the piano.

"I don't have a soprano," I told him nervously.

He smiled mischievously. "I know that."

"How do you know that? You've never heard me sing."

"You have the speaking voice of a well-schooled boy. Come along, it won't be so bad."

I sat down next to him on the piano bench. "You play," I said tensely.

"All right. Let's try this, shall we?" And he pointed to a song that I and everyone else in the room had known from the cradle.

I nodded and he began to play.

He had an absolutely wonderful tenor voice. Wouldn't you know it? I followed him, gaining confidence as we went along and adding volume as I became more sure of myself. Our voices fit together perfectly. When we had finished, he sat still for a moment, his hands on the keys. Then he turned his head a little and looked at me. I felt as if we had just made love.

"Good girl," he murmured, and I lowered my

eyes before he could read too much in them. Then the voices of the others broke in on us and once again the spell was broken.

How I loved him. It was all I could think of for the duration of the evening. When I was with him, I no longer felt lonely. It was as if a part of me, missing all of my life, had finally been found and I was whole again.

There would never be anyone else. I looked at Martin, at Lord Stowe. They were good men. Kind men. But they were not Diccon. I wondered bleakly what I was going to do with myself for the rest of my life.

21

I was waiting with Grandmama for our carriage to be brought around to the front of Brooks House when Lord Stowe asked if he could take me riding in the park the following morning.

"I am heartily sick of Hyde Park," I said forcefully. "I wish there was someplace I could gallop and gallop and gallop until I was dizzy."

"There's always Newmarket," said Martin's amused voice.

"Failing Newmarket, there is Richmond Park," said Lord Stowe. "You'd like Richmond, Miss Langley. It's out of the city and you can gallop all you want."

"It sounds wonderful," I said.

"You cannot go to Richmond without a

chaperone, Valentine," said Grandmama. "And I have no intention of taking part in such an all-day expedition."

"I'll take care of her, Aunt Mary," said Martin immediately.

"You are hardly a chaperon, my dear boy."

"Mama will come, won't you, Mama?" said Lady Barbara unexpectedly. I glanced at her in surprise and caught her giving me a distinctly dirty look. Clearly she did not like the idea of Martin spending an entire day in my company.

The duchess frowned and looked forbidding. She did not want Barbara to spend an entire day in Martin's company.

"I'll join you," said Diccon. "I would appreciate getting out into the country for the day also."

Martin gave Diccon a dirty look. "Why don't you return to Yorkshire, then?" he growled.

Diccon raised a black eyebrow. "I have business in London. Unfortunately."

"Why don't we send out the town crier and invite the rest of London?" Lord Stowe grumbled. He had not bargained on his ride in the park turning into such a parade of people.

Diccon smiled at the duchess. "Do say you will accompany us, Your Grace."

He was most unscrupulous, the way he used that smile.

The duchess melted like ice in the sun. "Of

course I will come, my lord, and I will bring my daughter."

Diccon's smile took on a tinge more radiance. "And you will engage to look after Miss Langley as well?"

"I should be delighted." The duchess gave me a benign look. She would be happy to have me along to keep Martin occupied. I stared at the marble floor of Brooks House's entry hall and thought that all these crosscurrents of purpose and emotion were getting extremely tedious.

It was a feeling that only became stronger as our party proceeded toward Richmond Park the following morning. I was so tired of it all—tired of Martin and his boring Barbara, tired of Lord Stowe and his reproachful looks, tired of Grandmama and Grandpapa and their attempts to push me into Martin's arms. I wished, with a fierceness that shook my whole being, that all these people would disappear and it would just be Diccon and I, galloping together as we had once done so often across the moors of Yorkshire.

Diccon was riding a big, well-muscled dark bay I had not seen before.

"Is he another horse you are schooling for a friend?" I asked curiously.

His face was unsmiling. "No. I bought this

fellow to hunt this winter. I rode him today because he needs the exercise."

Martin looked disapproving. "*Another* horse, my lord?"

"Horses are my extravagance," replied Diccon pleasantly, "as radical politics are yours."

Martin pokered up. "They are hardly my extravagance," he began.

"Enough!" I said loudly. "I am tired of listening to the two of you brangling. It is very tedious."

Diccon looked as if no one had ever scolded him in his life. Probably no one had—at least since he had left the schoolroom. Which was too bad; he needed a scolding once in a while. I stared at him repressively.

"Really, Val," Martin claimed my attention. "You sound as if we're two years old."

"You act two years old—the both of you."

Martin stuck his jaw out and glared at me. I turned back to Diccon and found him convulsed with internal mirth.

"What's so funny?" I asked austerely.

He ignored me. "Don't let her bait you, Wakefield," he advised.

Martin ignored Diccon. "Valentine, would you care to canter ahead for a little?"

"No," I said rudely, "I don't want to listen to your laments, Martin."

"Val!" He sounded really wounded. Too bad. I was heartily sick of his moonstruck conversations. I didn't relent, and after a minute he said stiffly, "I'll relieve you of my presence, then." Neither Diccon nor I said anything, and he trotted his horse up beside Barbara's. Barbara beamed and the duchess gave him a dirty look.

"You can't be thinking of marrying that pseudo-radical," Diccon said. "You'd end up doing his breathing for him."

For some reason this remark outraged me. "That's not true. And Martin is not a pseudo-anything. His political convictions are quite deeply felt."

"Then they do credit to his feelings, not his brain."

"Stop being so magisterial."

"Oh, Christ," said Diccon with exasperation.

"Are you enjoying the day, Miss Langley," asked Lord Stowe as he came up on the side of me Martin had left free.

Diccon said something under his breath and rode off precipitously.

The outing to Richmond looked to be turning out every bit as tedious as all the other affairs I had gone to in London. We dismounted to rest under some lovely trees and Martin talked to Barbara, Lord Stowe talked to me, and Diccon made himself charming to the duchess. In fact, he distracted her so successfully that she hardly noticed Martin monopolizing her daughter. I didn't understand his strategy at all.

We had tied the horses while we strolled about, and after a bit I went over to take a closer look at Diccon's bay. Diccon and Barbara came over to join me, and Diccon untied the bay and walked him a little for me.

"I'm getting tired," Barbara complained softly. "Isn't it time we started home, my lord?"

Barbara looked breathtakingly lovely in a blue velvet habit, but her riding ability was not in the same class as her looks. She was on a harmless-looking chestnut gelding that ambled along on a loose rein, obediently following whatever horse was next to him.

"Why don't you get on, Lady Barbara? I'm certain all the others will follow," I said. I took Diccon's reins, and without a word he went over to help her mount. As soon as Barbara was in the saddle, the duchess called imperiously.

"Come here a moment, Leyburn, please." Diccon started across the grass toward the rest of the group and away from the horses. I glanced over at Barbara.

"Look out, Lady Barbara," I said instantly, "there is a bee on your horse's flanks."

Too late. The gelding squealed, reared, and bolted. Barbara stayed on, but she had not been holding the reins securely and in the horse's frantic flight she lost them entirely. Barbara's scream was considerably more piercing than the gelding's had been.

I was standing holding the reins of Diccon's horse in my hands and without further thought I threw them over his neck, grabbed his mane in one hand and the front of the saddle in the other, and half-jumped, half-climbed onto the horse's back. I sent the bay after Barbara.

I could catch Barbara, I didn't have any doubt about that. The question was, Could I catch her before she fell off? The gelding was in full flight and Barbara looked distinctly unsteady in the saddle.

We were in a section of the park where the bridle path had the woods on one side and an open grassy field on the other. The path curved around the field in the manner of a great U. I reckoned that if I went across the field, I could cut Barbara off and stop the gelding from in front.

The problem was there was a five-foot fence around the field. Normally, of course, I wouldn't have hesitated to jump the fence, but today I was riding a strange horse, sitting astride in a skirt, which was hardly comfortable, and I had not the use of the stirrups. Diccon's were far too long for me to get my feet into. Also, there was very little space to put the horse at the fence because of the woods on the other side of the bridle path.

Oh, well. Diccon had said he planned to hunt the horse, so he must be a good jumper and at this rate Barbara was going to be off before I got to her. I pulled the bay up, tightened my legs, and put him at the fence.

He went over it like a dream. We galloped across the field and I felt intoxicated with the power I felt beneath me. For a few seconds I believe I quite forgot Barbara.

I remembered, however, as we approached the fence on the far side of the field, and I pulled the bay up a little as he would have to make a very fast turn once we landed so as not to crash into the woods. We sailed over the fence and negotiated the turn with a little more difficulty. Barbara was coming straight at us.

I put the bay directly across the path, and the gelding, seeing us, checked. Barbara lurched dangerously in the saddle. The silly fool was liable to fall if the gelding stopped too abruptly. I turned the bay in the direction Barbara was going and began to canter slowly. The gelding reached us and I planted the bay's rear end right in his face and began to slow down even more. The gelding slowed with us until we stopped. I removed the flapping reins from the gelding's neck and took them firmly into my possession.

"Come along," I said to Barbara, "I'll walk you back."

Barbara was received by her pale-faced mother

and an even paler-faced Martin. Martin lifted her off her horse and she collapsed, weeping, into his arms.

"That gelding is going to drop dead if we don't keep him walking," said Diccon.

"I know." I frowned. The poor old fellow's sides were heaving.

"You get on him, Valentine. I can't sit in that ridiculous sidesaddle."

"All right." I patted the bay's neck, which was slightly sweaty. "This fellow is marvelous, Diccon."

He laughed up at me. "You looked as if you were enjoying yourself."

I glanced guiltily over my shoulder at the hysterical Barbara, and then I grinned down at him.

"If you had taken that second fence at more of an angle, you wouldn't have had to wrench him around so much when you landed." He was right. It was an annoying habit of his.

"It was not having any stirrups that put me off a bit."

"Not to mention the skirt," he murmured, and stared at my leg. My skirt had pulled up far enough to expose the whole length of my high boot and my bare knee. "A very nice knee indeed," Diccon said admiringly.

I pulled my skirt down. He reached up, his eyes full of wicked laughter, and put his hands around my waist. I could feel his touch through the fabric of my jacket. He lifted me down, and when I risked a glance up at him again, the look on his face was quite serious. I went over to Barbara's horse and, without assistance, got into the saddle.

"Poor old fellow," I murmured, and patted the gelding's sweaty neck. I made him walk forward. "Poor love. You wore yourself out, didn't you? That's the boy, that's the fellow." The gelding put his head down and walked quietly around in a circle while Barbara was getting out her hysterics. Diccon walked the bay as well while we waited.

"I'm not getting back on," Barbara said at last.

"Of course you're going to get back on," Martin said soothingly. "Look—Valentine is riding him and he's as docile as a lamb."

"I know! I know!" Barbara said shrilly. "Valentine can do anything. Well, I can't, and I'm not getting back on that horse."

"He's half-dead, poor fellow," I said candidly. "You really ought to keep him in better condition, Lady Barbara."

Martin and the duchess both glared at me. The duchess herself rode like a sack of meal. Barbara evidently inherited her horsemanship from her mother; she certainly did not ride like a Bevil. I shouldn't have been at all surprised if that was why Diccon was so slow to make her an offer.

"I won't get on," Barbara repeated.

"How do you propose to get home, Barbara, if you don't ride?" asked Martin reasonably.

"You can hire a carriage for me at the nearest inn." Her great eyes looked even bluer awash in tears. "Please, Martin."

"Well . . ." said Martin, weakening.

"We will do nothing of the sort." It was Diccon's voice. "The horse is less than harmless. He only bolted because a bee stung him, and any rider with a grain of competence would have stopped him before he nearly ran himself into his grave. He doesn't have the energy to bolt should an entire hive of bees sting him at present. So please stop treating us to this very tedious Cheltenham tragedy and get into the saddle. Valentine, get off."

Nothing irritated Diccon more than people who were careless about the welfare of their animals—unless, of course, it was landlords who were careless of the welfare of their people. I got off.

"But I'm afraid," said Barbara in a small voice.

"Get on," said Diccon in the voice his ancestors had probably used to order faint-hearted knights into battle. He had clearly lost all patience with her. Barbara walked over to where I stood holding the gelding. He was still blowing. He had the sweetest face, and I rubbed his nose and murmured to him. With Martin's assistance,

Barbara got into the saddle; in a minute everyone else was mounted and we moved off.

Lord Stowe stuck to me like a plaster the whole way home, exclaiming over and over about my horsemanship. I made occasional noises to indicate I was listening to him, and Diccon, who rode on my other side, said absolutely nothing at all. From the look in his eye I gathered that if he had spoken it would have been to say something decidedly unpleasant, so I supposed it was best that he kept quiet. I wished Lord Stowe would do the same.

22

Two days after our Richmond Park outing, Lord Stowe asked me to marry him. Of course I said I couldn't and my refusal seemed to distress him a great deal. After he left, I was quite annoyed with myself. I shouldn't have allowed him to pay so much attention to me. Really, I was no hand at this business of suitors. I didn't want any suitors—except one, of course, and he had apparently disappeared.

Grandmama was delighted that I refused Lord Stowe. Her brain was teeming with visions of me as the next Lady Ardsley. I shouldn't have allowed Martin to talk me into acting out that particular charade with him. Now I was going to hurt Grandmama as well. I felt unutterably melancholy.

A week after Lord Stowe's proposal I was sitting at the piano working on Beethoven's "Sonata Pathetique," which wonderfully suited my mood, when Grandmama came into the room.

"Valentine," she said to me in a trembling voice, "Valentine, dear, may I speak to you for a few minutes?"

"Of course, Grandmama." I left the piano and went over to sit beside her on a sofa. Grandmama was looking ill and I bent toward her in concern. "What is it? Tell me, please."

Grandmama took my hand. "My very dear child, I find I scarcely know how to tell you this. But you must know." She stopped to breathe and panic struck my heart. Diccon, I thought irrationally. Something has happened to Diccon.

"It is about your cousin Martin," Grandmama resumed, and the icy fear in my chest disappeared. Of course, I thought, if anything happened to Diccon, no one would think to inform me.

"Yes?" I prompted as she stopped again.

"Oh, my dear, he has married Barbara Bevil."

"What!"

"Yes. He got a special license and they were married at his grandmother's home in Kent. The duke and duchess are furious, but there is nothing they can do now."

"Good God," I said rather feebly.

"You may well be amazed," returned Grandmama, pressing my hand tightly between her own. "He has behaved very badly, not only toward the Cartingtons but toward yourself. On *that* point, I can never forgive him."

The poor old dear was really upset for me. I thought for a few minutes and then said, "Grandmama, there is no need to be distressed for my sake. Believe me when I tell you that I don't love Martin, or at least not as a husband. I enjoy his company, but he has not wounded my heart."

"Are you being quite truthful, Valentine?"

"I am. I promise you."

She kissed me. "Your grandfather will be as relieved as I to hear this. On this point we have been wretched ever since Grandpapa heard the news at his club last night. It was our darling wish that you might be attached to each other—and we were persuaded that it was so. Imagine what we have been feeling on your account."

I felt most horribly guilty. I had known they would be disappointed by my failure to become Lady Ardsley, but I had not imagined this concern for my supposedly wounded heart.

"I have always felt Martin to be a very unsteady young man," Grandmama said now, and some of the old steel had returned to her voice, "but this has quite sunk him in my opinion."

"Now, Grandmama," I said placatingly. "Martin may not have behaved quite well on this occasion, but I have known him long enough to answer for his having many, many good qualities, and—"

"To elope!" cried Grandmama, not attending to me at all. "And with Barbara Bevil. I cannot believe it of her much as I might believe anything of *him*."

"She must love him excessively, I suppose. And really, Grandmama, it was very wrong of her parents to have opposed their marriage if that was the situation. There is nothing wrong with Martin. He is a pleasant, handsome, well-to-do young man, and one day he will be an earl."

"But not the Earl of Leyburn," said Grandmama dryly.

"Lord Leyburn had plenty of time to come up to scratch."

"Yes. He's back in Yorkshire, I understand."

"Oh."

Grandmama sighed. "Well, dear, the only comfort I can take from all this is that *you* have not been hurt."

"I am quite safe, Grandmama. And please do not cut Martin off from you again. He is Grandpapa's heir. Let us keep him as a friend."

Grandmama kissed me tenderly on the forehead. "My brave and generous girl. How like you to say that." She rose. "You will not mind going to the Bradshawes' ball this evening?"

"Of course not."

She gave me another speaking glance, testifying to my bravery, and went out of the room. I sat for several long minutes on the sofa.

So Diccon had gone home to Yorkshire. After a while I went back to the piano and for the remainder of the afternoon I played the most melancholy music I knew.

The end of the Season was nearly upon us. At the end of July most of the *ton* usually left town, either for the country or for Brighton. Grandmama asked me if I wished to go to Brighton, but I expressed a preference for Ardsley.

I was so very weary of London, of balls, of gossip, of people. I had to learn to live without Diccon, I knew that. Yet I thought I could make a better job of it in the country. I needed fresh air and quiet, and most of all, I needed my dogs and horses. When one felt like this, animals were really healing.

There were only a few more dances and assemblies and dinners to endure, and finally, it was the evening of the Countess of Rye's ball—the last ball of the Season. I let my maid array me in a thin ivory-colored gown and dress my hair with creamy white roses. I had lost weight in the last few weeks, and the gown had to be taken in. I had sworn Marie to secrecy. I didn't need Grandmama to start nagging at me to eat more.

There was a long line of carriages outside the door of the Ryes' Berkeley Square town house, and once we got inside, it took us half an hour to get up the stairs. The mingled smell of women's perfumes in the warm air made me feel faintly nauseous. How I longed for the clean, sharp air of the Dales!

I went along the receiving line, smiling and curtsying, and then on into the huge flower-filled ballroom. It was warm, too warm for all of these people to be crowded together indoors. It was a night to be out under the stars.

Grandmama had been very concerned for my social status after Martin's marriage. After all, I had refused two suitors and the third had married another woman, which left me bereft of my usual attendants. I didn't care if I sat and talked to the chaperones all night, but she and Grandpapa did, so I exerted myself to be pleasant to the dancing partners left me.

I was not deserted. In fact, I struck up a friendship with the Duke of Burford, who was having his first Season just as I was. He was extremely handsome and awesomely intelligent, and we got along very well. He had an understated sense of humor that I appreciated, and he found me entertaining. He said I reminded him of his young cousin.

Burford came over to me almost at once and we danced and then sat out a set, chatting comfortably. Grandmama was beginning to look at him hopefully, but I knew his interest in me was not romantic. We were becoming friends—and a friend was a great deal more valuable to me at the moment than another suitor whose feelings I would have to tiptoe around. I could say anything to Burford without fear of his misunderstanding me or thinking I meant more than I did. I think he felt the same about me. We were a great comfort to each other.

"Will you be going home for August, Your Grace?" I asked him now.

"Yes. I have quite a staggering amount of things to attend to."

I looked at him speculatively. "Do you have plans to go into government?"

"I sit in the Lords, of course, but do I want a minister's post? No. My main interest is mathematics, not politics. And for the moment, at least, the real business of government is still the land."

"That's what Lord Leyburn always says."

Burford raised an elegant eyebrow at my use of that name. "Well, he's right—for the moment. In fifty years it will be very different, however. Most people will be living in the cities."

"Factories," I said with loathing.

"Factories," he agreed. "It's progress, and it won't be stopped."

"Progress," I said with even greater loathing.

Burford smiled. "You do sound like a disciple of Leyburn."

"On the subject of factories, I am."

"You may as well try to hold the planets from their appointed rounds as try to hold back progress, Miss Langley." Quite suddenly he laughed. "Although if anyone could do it, Leyburn is the man."

"How?" I asked curiously.

"Sheer force of personality," he retorted, and we both laughed.

"Val!" said a voice at my elbow. "Here you are! I've been looking for you."

"Martin!" I turned and grinned at him. "Congratulations. Where is your bride?"

"She's dancing with Rye." He picked my hand up and kissed it. "You are a genius, cousin," he said, "but don't tell Barbara."

"I won't. I haven't told Grandmama either, so I am afraid you are in her black books again." I added ruthlessly, "Better you than me."

He chuckled. "You must help me bring her around."

Burford had courteously drawn back while this cousinly exchange was going on, but now he laid a hand on my arm.

"I rather believe someone is looking for you, Miss Langley."

I looked up, my eyes drawn as if by magnets to the door. There, staring at me across the glittering crowd, was Diccon.

23

The orchestra was playing and the floor was filled with dancing couples. Diccon walked straight across it, ignoring the protests of the dancers whom he disturbed. I watched him coming—we all did—and it was as if something fierce, masculine, and beautiful, like a panther, had been let loose in the civilized confines of the ballroom. He came on, unwaveringly, and as he reached us, I saw that his eyes were now on Martin.

Martin looked frightened and I couldn't blame him.

"You goddamn bastard," said Diccon quietly.

Martin flushed deeply and then became very pale. He opened his mouth to speak, failed, and

then tried again. "Barbara loves me, my lord,"
he managed—quite bravely, I thought.

"Barbara! Who the hell cares about Barbara.
It's Valentine you've hurt, you . . ." Well, I won't
repeat the words Diccon used. Suffice it to say
they were not appropriate for a ballroom.

"Valentine!" said Martin in genuine astonishment, and looked at me.

"My heart is not broken, Diccon," I began.

"What do you mean, your heart is not
broken?" He turned on me, eyes narrowed.

"Er—I believe you are beginning to attract
some undue notice, my lord," Burford said
softly. "Might I suggest you and Miss Langley go
out onto the terrace and finish your conversation
there?"

Diccon transferred his attention to the speaker.
"Burford," he said. "By God, as soon as my back
is turned . . ."

I looked around me and saw that we were
indeed the center of interest for almost the entire
ballroom. "Good God," I said faintly. Thank
heavens Burford had noticed.

"Diccon," I said firmly, "come out on the
terrace with me. Everyone is staring at us."

Diccon turned his head and stared back.
Everyone suddenly began to talk again. I had to
stifle a giggle at the look on Martin's face. Suddenly I felt very very happy.

"Come along," I said. "I'll explain everything. But not here." Diccon gave Martin and then Burford a look that probably kept them awake for weeks and then he turned and followed me across the floor and out the French doors to the terrace. Everyone pretended not to watch us go.

The terrace had steps leading down into a small garden, and we walked as far away from the house as we could go before stopping.

"All right," he said then. The moon illuminated the blackness of his hair; his eyes were shadowed and dark. "Let's hear it."

"You cannot blame Martin for marrying Lady Barbara," I said reasonably. "You had well over a year to make her an offer and you did not."

He spoke very slowly and clearly. "Barbara is a bloody bore and she sits a horse like a sack of potatoes."

"I agree completely, Diccon. But Martin thinks she's wonderful and she loves him back, you see, but her papa wanted her to marry *you*. So Martin and I decided to make her so jealous she would agree to elope with him."

There was a long, rather unnerving silence. "Are you telling me that all the time you and he were billing and cooing like two doves in a nest, you were only *pretending?*"

I swallowed. "Er, well, yes."

There was another silence. "Then I see I

wasted my time in coming here." His voice sounded very cool, very distant, but I was watching his hands.

"Diccon," I asked softly, *"why* did you come?"

Silence.

I stepped closer to him. "I don't love Martin," I said. "And I turned down Lord Henry and Lord Stowe. There is only one man in the world for me. Surely you know that."

"Valentine." Astonishingly, he sounded uncertain.

I looked up at him in the moonlight. "Am I wrong?" I asked. "Don't you care?"

"Valentine," he said again. "Christ, Valentine." And he bent his head and kissed me.

He had kissed me once before, a gentle and tender kiss, the sort of kiss one uses to reassure a frightened child. This kiss was quite relentlessly adult, and it left me breathless and trembling. It also seemed to convince him of my own feelings.

"I didn't know," he said after a bit. "You ran away from me, refused to marry me."

"But that was because you felt you *had* to marry me. I loved you far too much to do that to you."

"I didn't know. I didn't understand. I still thought of you as a child, I suppose."

We had found a bench to sit down on. Or at

least Diccon was sitting on the bench. I was sitting on his lap.

"When did you change your mind?" I asked curiously.

He kissed my hair. "I missed you like hell after you'd gone. I made everyone's life miserable at Carlton. Finally, Ned said that you were in London and recommended that I go and see how you were doing. I think he knew what was wrong with me better than I did."

Darling, darling Mr. Fitzallan.

"So I followed his advice." I could hear the smile in his voice. "Christ, were they glad to see me go at home!"

I chuckled and kissed the line of his jaw. "Go on."

The smile completely left his voice. "I was so unforgivably vain, Valentine. I thought I would see you, and perhaps, if we still got along as we used to, I would ask you to marry me again." A note of savage mockery crept into his voice. "You had hero-worshiped me; I knew that. I hadn't counted on your growing out of such a childish emotion. I just assumed you would still think me as wonderful as you used to."

I kissed the other side of his jaw.

"It didn't take me long to realize that you were not the boy-child I remembered. You were a woman—the woman I wanted. But by then I didn't think you wanted me. God, how I longed to put a bullet through Wakefield!"

"Poor Martin," I murmured. "You were so nasty to him."

"I was the pattern of chivalry compared to what I wanted to do to him!"

I kissed his ear. "I had no idea you were jealous."

"I was nearly out of my mind with jealousy. And not just of Wakefield. It's finally what drove me out of London."

"How could you—*you*, of all people—have been so unperceptive?" I kissed his other ear.

"But you are enough, don't you see," Diccon said through his teeth, "to drive a man mad!"

Five minutes later he unceremoniously pushed me off his lap and stood up. "If we don't get out of here very shortly," he said, "I won't answer for the consequences." He sounded almost as shaken as I felt.

I smoothed my dress with trembling hands. The roses had all fallen out of my hair and I tried to pin them back in again.

"We'll emulate Cousin Martin and get a special license," Diccon said.

"All right." I was afraid the roses were crooked, but to be truthful, I didn't much care.

"How pleased Robert and Georgie will be." The amused note in his voice told me he had regained his composure.

We started to walk toward the house. "What will Mr. Fitzallan say?"

"I don't think he'll be surprised at all. Ned knows me pretty well."

As we walked in the French doors of the ballroom, the orchestra stopped playing. It seemed as if a thousand eyes turned immediately toward us.

"Valentine!" said Grandmama. She looked at my hair and frowned direly.

"How nice to see you, Lady Ardsley," Diccon said. He gave her his best smile. "Valentine and I are going to be married."

It was just like him to inform her like that. It probably never crossed his mind to ask.

Grandmama, I am sorry to say, looked absolutely delighted. "Married!" she echoed. She looked at me. "To Lord Leyburn!"

"The one and only," I said dryly, and next to me Diccon chuckled.

"Oh, my dear child." Grandmama kissed me. "I always knew you would make a brilliant marriage." She beamed at Diccon.

"Martin!" she called imperiously, and my cousin, accompanied by his bride, came over to join us. Both newlyweds looked nervously at Diccon.

"Lord Leyburn and Valentine are going to be married," Grandmama informed them smugly.

"By Jove!" Martin looked thunderstruck.

"I'm so sorry your grandfather wasn't well enough to accompany us this evening," Grandmama said to me regretfully.

"We are going to get a special license," Diccon told Grandmama. "It seems quite the thing these days." It bothered him not at all that every eye in the room was on him.

Grandmama stiffened her back. "I have my heart set on Valentine's being married from Ardsley Church."

"She can be married from anywhere you like, Lady Ardsley," Diccon said pleasantly, "but she is going to be married next week."

Grandmama looked terribly upset, and Barbara and Martin exchanged speaking looks. I realized, with a sudden jolt, what they were thinking.

Poor Grandmama. And I rather felt as if I owed her a wedding. I put my hand on her arm.

"Two months," I said. "We will be married in two months. And you may make all the arrangements, Grandmama." I looked at Diccon. "Everyone will be counting on their fingers if we get married immediately," I said.

He frowned. "Dammit, it's your virtue I'm concerned about. Do you expect me to keep my hands off you for two more months?"

I thought of our recent interlude in the garden and saw his point. Grandmama and Barbara looked scandalized. Martin grinned.

"You'll have to go home to Yorkshire for a while," I said.

"What!"

"Yes." I smiled at him. "It's the only way, Diccon."

"Christ, what do I care what everyone thinks?"

He didn't care at all, of course. Neither did I, actually, but poor Grandmama did. And she had been terribly good to me.

"Two months," I said inexorably, stepped on his toe, and looked meaningfully at Grandmama.

"Oh, all right," he gave in. "I'll paint the bedroom for you."

I opened my mouth to answer and noticed that everyone in the vicinity had their ears tilted our way.

"That will be just lovely," I said sweetly. "Why don't we go into the supper room and get something to eat? I'm starving."

"You should be. You look as if you've just been through a famine." Diccon frowned at me. "Haven't you been eating?"

"No. I've been pining. But now I'm hungry." I put my hand on his arm. "Come along, Diccon."

As we moved off together, I heard Martin say to my grandmother, "Val will keep him in order, ma'am. There's nothing that girl is afraid of."

Diccon heard him too and gave me a long, dark

look that set my pulses racing. He bent his head toward mine.

"Are you going to keep me in order, Valentine?"

I gazed up at him and felt weak in the knees. "No," I said very softly. "I'm going to love you."

"But not for two months?"

I sighed. "But not for two months."

He smiled at me, very faintly. "Come along," he said, "and I'll stuff you full of lobster patties. I never have liked skinny women."

JOIN THE REGENCY READERS' PANEL

Help us bring you more of the books you like by filling out this survey and mailing it in today.

. Book title:_____

Book #:_____

. Using the scale below how would you rate this book on the following features.

Poor	Not so Good		O.K.			Good		Excellent	
1	2	3	4	5	6	7	8	9	10

Rating

Overall opinion of book......................._____
Plot/Story ...._____
Setting/Location ...._____
Writing Style ...._____
Character Development ...._____
Conclusion/Ending ...._____
Scene on Front Cover ...._____

. On average about how many romance books do you buy for yourself each month?_____

. How would you classify yourself as a reader of Regency romances?
I am a ( ) light ( ) medium ( ) heavy reader.

. What is your education?
( ) High School (or less)   ( ) 4 yrs. college
( ) 2 yrs. college   ( ) Post Graduate

. Age_____   7. Sex: ( ) Male ( ) Female

Please Print Name_____

Address_____

City_____State_____Zip_____

Phone # (   )_____

Thank you. Please send to New American Library, Research Dept, 1633 Broadway, New York, NY 10019.